Frederic W. Putnam

Sketch of Hon. Lewis H. Morgan

Frederic W. Putnam

Sketch of Hon. Lewis H. Morgan

ISBN/EAN: 9783337011352

Printed in Europe, USA, Canada, Australia, Japan

Cover: Foto ©Andreas Hilbeck / pixelio.de

More available books at **www.hansebooks.com**

MEXICAN LETTERS

WRITTEN

DURING THE PROGRESS OF THE LATE WAR

BETWEEN THE

UNITED STATES

AND

MEXICO,

BY

B. H. M. BRACKENRIDGE:

NOW COLLECTED AND REPUBLISHED, WITH NOTES AND CORRECTIONS, TO BE
COMPLETED IN TWO NUMBERS.

Genus audax Japeti.

WASHINGTON:
PRINTED BY ROBERT A. WATERS.
1850.

PREFACE.

One who thinks for himself, is very apt to think alone, or with a minority, especially in our free republic, where there is such proneness in opinion to run into party. The individual is restrained by party trammels from asserting his independence, and he must adopt all the articles of political, as well as religious creeds, or be expelled from the church. Although agreeing with the whigs generally, I could not agree with them in our late war with Mexico, that justice was on the side of that republic; still less could I approve of the constant condemnation of the war in which we were engaged. I applied the same principle to that war that I did to the late war with Great Britain, that is to say, that it becomes every citizen to sustain his country against the common enemy, both by word and deed.

The letters now collected and submitted to the public, were written in this spirit. The author has endeavored to treat with respect the opinions of those who differed from him. He does not think he can be justly censured by any one for attempting to prove by fair and honest reasoning, that his country

was in the right, and the enemy in the wrong. He
may be condemned by his party at the present day,
but at a future day the judgment may be reversed.
These letters may serve as materials for history.
There will be no difficulty in finding the records of
the arguments of the administration party, which pro-
moted and defended the war; or of the opposition,
which denounced it. But before making up a ver-
dict, the voice of the small number dissenting from
the latter ought also to be heard. It is with this
view chiefly, that these letters are collected and pre-
served. There is, besides, usually a freshness in
the commentaries on contemporary or passing events,
which cannot be attained by historical compilation,
however elegant and philosophic, while the former,
may be but rude and unpolished.

The author, although desirous of the annexation
of Texas, was fearful of the consequences of any acquisition of territory on our southern borders, for the
single reason, that it might endanger the harmony of
the Union. He foresaw great evils and dangers arising from the *quasi* independence of Texas, and
from the certainty of the occupation of Upper California by Great Britain, in case it did not fall into our
hands. Looking into the future, both of these points
presented the probability of fearful collisions with
that power. We had a Scylla and Caribdis before
us; our bark could not strike upon both; but
whether it will escape both, the Almighty, who has
thus far favored us in a peculiar manner, can alone

determine. As 'to Mexico, I have long been of opinion, that we could never have a peace on a lasting foundation, without a war. If that neighboring and jealous people had still remained united to the Spanish monarchy, it would have been the same thing. This event was but removed farther off, or postponed by the acquisition of Louisiana and the Mississippi, but soon or late, a collision was inevitable; and nothing else would determine the terms on which we should live in future, as neighbors. To other persons, all this may appear visionary and idle, the mere dreams of the closet. Be it so—let my opinions pass for what they are worth; they are, at least, those of a thinker, an observer, and an actor on the scene.

LETTER 1.

Justice on the side of Texas in her war with Mexico.

JUNE, 1846.

To the Editor of the Commercial Journal :

We continually meet with the phrases in newspapers, English and American, and especially in Mexican documents, " the robbery and plunder of Mexico, of her province of Texas," and of the "ingratitude of the people of Texas." These expressions, from frequent use, have come to have some meaning attached to them with those who are not acquainted with the true history of the case. Now what is Mexico, and what particular right had she ever to Texas? She was once a vice-royalty of Spain, composed of various Intendencies, or local and subordinate Governments. These Intendencies, taking advantage of the troubles of old Spain, set up for themselves, and endeavored to throw off the Spanish dominion, practising the same thing that Texas has done as respects Mexico ; and if Texas has been ungrateful to Mexico, for the same reason Mexico has been ungrateful to Spain. But the struggle for independence was carried on by them separately, and independently of each other; not united like the British Colonies in the Revolutionary War. It may be new to some to be told that Texas not only achieved her own independence without the aid of any Mexican Province or Intendency, but was actually the means, through the Americans then inhabiting the country, with the aid of citizens of the United States, of enabling the other Mexican Provinces to gain *their* independence. Before I am done this will be demonstrated. Mexico owes a debt to the American people of Texas and of the United States, for her independence, *if it be worth anything*, and, consequently, the ingratitude is on her side. But her efforts were finally successful through the treachery of Iturbide. He was a traitor to Spain, in whose employment he was, and by one of those military revolts, since of daily recurrence in the mis-named Republic of Mexico, overturned the Spanish authority, and proclaimed himself Emperor! The empire was soon after overturned by something approaching nearer to a popular revolution in the Intendencies or Provinces. An attempt at something like a Republic, followed the downfall of the Emperor. States were formed out of the Intendencies, and a confederated Republic, in imitation of the United States, was established in form, but in form only. Texas, with parts of two other Intendencies, was constituted one of these States. The confederated Republic was not long lived. It fell to pieces or was overturned by the military chiefs, and then each State, was again compelled to look out for itself. Some submitted, some were subdued by this military power, the only real power; and others still retain their preference for the federative system, although compelled to submit to the central authority. The only one which *did not submit to the overthrow of the Constitution by a military usurper, was ungrateful Texas.*

Santa Anna, after having expelled Iturbide, next overturned the federative system, restored the central power of the city of Mexico, and at the same time grasped the substance of absolute power, prudently avoiding the name of Emperor. Troops were sent to Texas, and these *ungrateful* people were generously called upon, *to give up their religion and surrender their rifles!* The consequence was, that Coss and his fourteen hundred men were driven over the Rio Grande. People talk of the Texans having no cause of war, now I ask any one, who has a drop of American blood in his veins, to say, what he would think of an order by a military despot, to the people of Alleghany county for instance, *to give up their religion and their arms?* But then did not Mexico make grants of land to these ungrateful American settlers, and did not that entitle her to call upon those settlers to comply with her moderate requests ?* It is true, Mexico did make grants of land in Texas ; yes, of land which did not belong to her, for they were won from Spain by the Texan Americans themselves, who constituted nine tenths of the people of that part of the country. And

* Terms of reproach like these have been applied to the Texans, even from the pulpit, by learned divines, who are better theologians, than jurists or statesmen. As moral men, they ought to beware how they cast reproach on their neighbors, without being sure of their facts ; and even then, tempered by charity. If the allusion is to the grants of land made by Mexico, those grants were made from the most interested motives. Texas contained but two small towns, San Antonio and Nacogdoches ; all the rest was a wilderness, wandered over by the Camanches and Lipans, and other hostile Indians, with the exception of the few American settlements formed by hardy American pioneers, and maintained by the rifle, at the constant risk of life. The object of the Mexican Government was to cover their frontier from Indian depredations by placing an advanced guard of our countrymen between them and their savage enemies. The lands of Texas were worse than useless and worthless to Mexico, because they merely served as the place of refuge for her savage enemies ; she, in fact, gave nothing that was of any value to her ; on the contrary, the grants were intended for her own advantage and security. But for these settlements, her whole frontier would have been laid waste ; and many a bloody battle was fought, and many a Texan life was lost in the border war of which the Mexican Provinces reaped the benefit. But for the Texans, it is difficut to say, what would have been the condition of the internal provinces at this day. After expending millions in money and labor—after opening farms, building towns, and rearing vast herds of cattle, the Mexicans begin to discover its value, and conceived the idea of placing their peon slaves on the improved lands, which were to be parcelled out among military chiefs. Besides, the sturdy republican predelections of the Americans settled in Texas, and their intelligence, were annoying to the leaders of the military despotism of Mexico. It was conceived, that the purpose for which they were invited to take possession of the dangerous post of frontier settlers, was now accomplished, and that their further services could be dispensed with ; and, at the same time, gratify the cupidity of their military chieftains. It was they who were frustrated in the *attempt to steal the Texan lands*, while the Texans did nothing more than defend their own—that which they had created, *and which had never been the property of Mexico.*

what was the next movement on the part of Mexico? These grants were made during the federative system—Americans were invited on account of their valuable assistance in contending against the Spanish monarchy, and guarding the frontier against hostile Indians—but when they were no longer needed, when the lands improved by them, tempted the cupidity of the military despots, and when their sturdy habits of independence and love of liberty stood in the way of the despotic schemes of the military aspirants and plunderers of Mexico, the next thing was to expel, or exterminate, the ungrateful and hated North Americans. Santa Anna marched at the head of ten thousand men for this holy purpose. We may judge of the humane and civilized spirit of these barbarians, (for whom so much sympathy is ignorantly felt by some of our fellow citizens,) by the murder of Fanning and four hundred American Texans in cold blood, after a surrender as prisoners of war! This more than diabolical atrocity, is scarcely equalled by the murder of the Huguenots by the fanatical ruffian, Pedro Menendez.

I am disgusted when I hear persons talk of the injured Mexicans, when such butcheries as these are passed *in almost approving silence.* But Santa Anna met, not indeed *with the fate he deserved,* but such an overthrow, as every true lover of liberty and political justice ought to desire. His forces were driven across the Rio Grande ; Texas declared her independence ; she successfully maintained it, and proclaimed the Rio Grande as her boundary, and has devolved that *claim* upon us. Upon this mere outline of facts, I appeal to every just and unprejudiced, unbigoted man, to say, how has Texas been ungrateful to Mexico, and how have we, or Texas, been guilty of robbing Mexico of an independent State, which has fairly united her fate with ours? Mr. Webster says, Mexico is "the most ill-governed country on earth ;" and I will add, that her Government is the most faithless, unprincipled, and cruel. For the honor of humanity, there are noble exceptions, doubtless, among the people and her public officers, nevertheless, such, with too much truth, is the general character of both.

In 1812, a young man of the name of Magee, who had been a Lieutenant in the Unsted States service, after resigning for the purpose, assembled a force of American riflemen between the Sabine and the Trinity Rivers, and raised the standard of revolt against Spain, ostensibly under a native named Bernardo. At this time, the different attempts at revolution throughout the vice-royalty, had been completely put down, and the last rebel, Hidalgo, publicly executed. Magee took Nacogdoches, then marched to La Bahia, where, with four hundred Americans, he withstood a siege of three months, the American riflemen making such havoc among the Spanish soldiers in their occasional sorties, that their commander was compelled to raise the siege and retreat to St. Antonio ; Magee, in the meantime died, not more than twenty-two years of age. The Americans, in all, about three hundred, and one hundred Indians, pursued the royal troops until within twelve miles of St. Antonio. Here they were drawn up twelve hundred strong, with six pieces of artillery. A charge was made by the American riflemen, the artillery taken ; and on the same day they took possession of the town. About six months after this, General Elisondo, with sixteen hundred men, who had approached the place, was attacked by the Americans with about nine hundred, (three or four hundred of them native Texans,) and completely routed. Two Spanish armies were thus entirely destroyed. A third, under Arredondo, would have shared the same fate, but for the desertion of Manchaco who led the Texan Spaniards.

It thus appears, that the revolutionary fire was kept alive in Texas when every where else extinguished. It was the means of exciting other revolutionary attempts in different parts of Mexico. Even after Texas was reduced by the Spanish troops, new attempts were continually made by Americans, and with partial success, to regain it. It was, through the medium of

Texas, that supplies were continually obtained to aid the Mexicans in all their struggles for independence. Hundreds of Americans sacrificed their lives in every part of Mexico in support of the cause. In the unfortunate expedition of General Mina, not less than three hundred Americans embarked, few of whom ever returned. I am well convinced that without the aid of the ungrateful Texans, in the supply of men, arms, and means of war, Mexico could not have gained her independence. And what was the return made to the citizens of the United States for this, and for being first to take her by the hand, and recognize her as an independent Republic? It was natural for Americans to sympathize with their countrymen in Texas when oppressed by Mexico, and a determination avowed to exterminate them; and hence, the principal cause of offence to Mexico, which instigated the shocking treatment of American citizens engaged in their lawful pursuits in that country, under the faith of treaties. Nothing was more common than the imprisonment of Americans in the horrid prisons of Mexico; for personal liberty, which to us, is the dearest thing on earth; with them, is the cheapest. Our trade with Mexico was almost annihilated. In every instance in which American vessels were seized under some frivolous pretext as an excuse for plunder, every one on board was thrown into prison among the vilest malefactors, and compelled, for an indefinite period, to undergo every kind of suffering, under which a large proportion actually perished. A stupid and barbarous prejudice—a fiendish hostility, seems to prevail among the] great body of that people where no opportunity has been afforded of becoming personally acquainted with us. It reminds one of the ignorant self-conceit and arrogance of the Chinese, and there seems to be no way of securing their esteem and respect, but by adopting the course pursued by the English with the "Celestials." Our long forbearance has doubtless tended to encourage this insolence. They received a timely check from the French when the castle of Ulloa was battered down with so little ceremony, and the authorities required to pay on the deck of Admiral Baurin's vessel, a million of dollars, as the estimated value of their plunder of French subjects. They now entertain a high opinion of French civilization and politeness. England has always held them under her thumb, by loans, investments, and cajolery, and they now look to her for aid, support, and sympathy. England has a deep stake in Mexico; it is to be expected therefore, that she will sympathize with *her own interests;* that she will do all she can to excite against us the prejudices of the Mexicans, exhibiting our conduct through a jaundiced medium, both to Mexicans and Europeans. No pains will be spared to place us before the world as in the wrong in this contest. American editors ought to be on their guard against such partial and interested representations as that of J. D. Powell's, "Chairman of the South American and Mexican Association," as well as against the low and scurrilous slanders of the British presses of Montreal.

H. M. BRACKENRIDGE.

LETTER 2.

The first blow of the War—Fortunate result—Reflections.

JULY, 1846.

Never was a country more suddenly raised up from a state of depression, to the most enthusiastic rejoicing and gladness, than we have been since the late glorious intelligence from the Rio Grande! We may talk about the justice of the war, and there may be fanatics who would rejoice in the defeat of our armies, but the people, true to patriotic feeling, rejoice with one heart over the glorious achievements of our countrymen. We are the same people that we were at the capture of Cornwallis, and at the defeat of the British at New Orleans.

There was a gloom settling over the public mind, and fears

began to be entertained of news like that from Detroit, at the opening of that unfortunate campaign. To all appearance, General Taylor and his gallant army were shut up in Fort Brown, and suddenly cut off by an overwhelming force of Mexicans, from his military depot at Point Isabel. If that depot, defended by less than a thousand men, its fortifications incomplete, should be assailed by the whole force of Arista and Ampudia, its safety appeared to be hopeless. If taken, the army of General Taylor, shut up in Fort Brown, with supplies only for a few weeks, would be either compelled to surrender, or attempt to retreat to Corpus Christi. The consequences, in either case, would be a triumph for the Mexican arms, fatal to all hope of peace.

I passed some sleepless nights in revolving the subject in my mind. The idea constantly recurred to me, as a sort of waking dream, that General Taylor would leave a force in Fort Brown and with the main body of his army cut his way to Point Isabel. I was disposed to blame him for suffering himself to be separated from his depot of supplies; but the war itself came on him suddenly, and he was obliged to *wait the first blow*. In this feverish state of mind, a friend came to my house early one morning with two newspaper slips containing the accounts of the two battles of Palo Alto, and Resaca. Never was the anxiety of a people more suddenly and joyfully relieved! It was like the anxiety felt by a family for the fate of those nearest and dearest to it. We are peculiarly a national people; for every man has a share in the Government; feels an interest in it, as a part owner, and he feeels his own safety and honor embarked in the same bottom with the safety and honor of the nation.

Thank God, we are safe! They must be very short sighted men who could wish success to the Mexicans. We should have had scenes of bloodshed and devastation unparalleled. Our preparations for war' would have had to be renewed on a vast and expensive scale; the most extravagant hopes in the presumptuous and barbarous enemy would have been encouraged; while even the Sabine, for a boundary, would not have contented them. Their demands would have known no bounds, and the prospects of peace, would have been remote indeed. Now, humbled and broken, their country exposed to invasion and conquest, if we only will it; undeceived in their fancied military pre-eminence, they must be insane if they do not hasten to sue for peace. I confess, I did not look for such decided success in the first blow, which, in wars and battles, is often so important; and that, over a people who have been continually practising the art of war, and who ought to excel in it, if they can excel in any thing. If the history of nations be a history of battles, (as it is said to be) Mexico will claim a conspicuous page in that history. European nations, who have been in the habit of judging others, chiefly by their military prowess, will open their eyes when they receive the news; for they have already prognosticated according to their wishes, that we must be disgraced in the trial of arms with Mexico.

I have no doubt, that President Polk will lay hold of this occasion to offer terms of peace. I am not one of those whigs who believe, that it was the predetermined plan of this administration to involve the country in a war with Mexico. I rather accuse them of a want of foresight, as to the inevitable result of the annexation of Texas. If they had been convinced, that war would have been the consequence of that measure, I honestly think, there would have been no annexation. The repeated declarations, that it would not be followed by war, I believe, were made in sincerity. For my part, I thought differently; the issue seemed to me to be this—shall we take Texas, *and war*, or leave the numerous questions of policy arising out of the independence of Texas, to take care of themselves, and our relations with Mexico to remain in the same embroiled state for an indefinite period? There is a providence in the affairs of men, which shapes their fortunes, " rough hew them as they will."

I neither approve nor condemn the course of the administration in relation to this war. I am convinced it would not, intentionally, endanger its popularity on such rocks and shoals, as the expense and casualty of war necessarily present. A demonstration was thought to be sufficient to secure the advantages of a treaty of peace and limits, settling all our differences, and gratifying the nation, by a great acquisition of terri-tory. A small share of the glory and popularity which may attend this war, will be reaped by the administration! These will be bestowed on those who are immediately engaged on the scene of action. Our friends are doing all they can to make it Mr. Polk's war ; but the people will persist in looking upon it, as General Scott's and General Taylor's war ; so far, at least, as the glory is concerned ; if it should prove disastrous, then, indeed, the administration will come in for a share.

LETTER 3.

` *The annexation of Texas, the unavoidable cause of war—The energetic prosecution of the war the only way to obtain peace.*

SEPTEMBER, 1846.

SIR : If the editor of the " Commercial Journal," will look over his files he will find, that two years ago I gave my opinion, that the annexation of Texas would not merely *lead* to war, but would be war—that it would be a long war, and that if we carried the war into Mexico, would require an addition to our regular force of at least thirty thousand men, and an annual expenditure of thirty millions of dollars. I ask you whether my prediction has not been fulfilled ? Yet, you must suppose, that I say this from friendship to Mexico ; I have no sympathy with either her people or her military despotism. I feel interested in the honor of my own country, and all my hopes and wishes are for the success of her arms.

I do, moreover, honestly believe, that as respects Mexico, our cause is just. Whether it was within the scope of possibility for the Government, (I mean the whole Government, not the Executive branch alone,) by prudent measures, and by forbearance, to avoid hostilities, is a question which I do not choose to discuss at present. But I contend, that Texas had a right to annex herself to the United States, if she chose; that we neither violated any right of Mexico nor any treaty stipulation in accepting the offer, although, there is no doubt that, looking at things as they actually exist, the joint resolution of Congress annexing Texas would, inevitably be followed by war.

Mexico has rejected, and continues to reject, all overtures of peace, excepting on the condition of our retiring beyond the Sabine, and making compensation for the wrong alleged to have been done her, by the annexation and military occupation of her province of Texas. Having thus got into war in consequence of this step, the war has become the act of the nation, and there is no hope of peace without concessions, which we cannot make. It is useless for highly sublimated moralists, and highly honorable statesman, to propose such concessions—every one knows, as a matter of mere fact, that the nation will not consent to them. We are in for the war, and must fight it out. Judging of nations and men as they are, and not, perhaps, as they ought to be, there is no other course...

Besides, there are points in which we are bound by positive obligations, not by mere abstract morality. We are bound to maintain the right of Texas to the boundary of the Rio Grande, and we are bound to secure the amount of spoliations due by the Mexican Government to our own citizens. As we are now at war, (and it is not material as to this, whether by our act, or that of Mexico,) the payment of that debt must be secured by sequestration of California or other territory, and at the same

3

time, there must be indemnity for the expenses of the war. As to the prospects ahead, that is, as to the results of the war, they do not appear to me encouraging, and as to the prospects of peace, they are still more gloomy.

I believe there is no nation on the Globe more powerful for defence, than we are. But our power for warlike conquest, is an idea which ought not to be encouraged, and no people had ever less necessity for it. In order to be conquerors, we must have regular standing armies; we must have tributary provinces as Rome had; and, consequently, a system incompatible with our simple democratic republican institutions. Unoccupied countries, like California, may be conquered by our settlements, as Texas and some of our States were conquered. In the course of time, the whole of North America, and, perhaps South America, will gradually and imperceptibly, yield to this kind of conquest. But at present, the countries beyond the Rio Grande are inhabited by a different race of people, too numerous to be at once absorbed or displaced, and whose habits and character do not fit them to become integral portions of our confederacy. Mere dependencies and colonies do not suit the spirit of our free institutions.

The western side of the Rio Grande presents a very different case from that of Texas, settled by our own people, and which but a few years ago was little better than a wilderness, a frontier to Mexico, as well as to us. The States of New Leon, Coawilla, and Tamaulipas, contain half a million of people, have been settled two hundred years, and contain ancient cities and towns. They are spread over a surface as large as Virginia and the Carolinas, and backed by other more extensive States towards Mexico. If the struggle lay only between the Mexican military and our armies, a few decisive battles might end the contest. But we have to overcome the prejudices, ignorance, and antipathies of the population, a conquest a thousand times more difficult than that of arms. And are we certain that the people of those States will remain perfectly passive, and that their countrymen beyond the Sierra Madre, cannot be rendered formidable as guerrillas? Our estimate of them may be too low. In case of some severe reverse, their numbers, should they rise en masse, may overwhelm detached bodies of our troops. The proclamation of Ampudia, denouncing as traitors, all who will hold intercourse with our people, has had its effect. The people will become exasperated at the outrages which will, in all probability, be committed by our irregular troops, and the guerrilla warfare will bristle over the whole country. Few among us are aware of its vast extent. It is for the greater part composed of barren mountains and arid plains, interspersed with fertile valleys, and entirely unlike our western States. We will have to guard a frontier of two thousand miles, from Santa Fee to Matamoras, without mentioning California. We will have to garrison all the principal towns between the Rio Grande and the Sierra Madre. If we attempt to advance beyond Monterey, we must force our way through a population of several millions, after crossing a desert of several hundred miles. Conquests are easy enough, when people are willing to be conquered, but when they determine to resist, it is a very different matter. When Napoleon attempted the conquest of Spain, after the manner that Edward I undertook that of Scotland, he had possession of Madrid and all the principal cities, with five hundred thousand of the best troops in the world, and yet, in less than three years, his Generals were driven out with a remnant of thirty thousand men! The capture of Burgoyne and of Cornwallis, show what a critical thing it is for an invading army to penetrate an enemy's country, with the wave of an unconquered people closing behind them. Our armies are about to operate in a country without roads, without supplies or resources, through defiles, over deserts without water, and under a burning sun. I have great confidence in them, and I believe that whatever can be done, they will do; but shall not expect impossibilities of them. They may reach and take Mon-terey, after hard fighting and much suffering, and then be com-pelled, by superior numbers, to fall back on the Rio Grande, and fortifying themselves, carry on a war of detachments with little prospect of any definitive result. There is no hope of bringing the war to a speedy close without putting in the field at least twenty thousand regulars and thirty thousand volunteers, and their advancing from Monterey and Vera Cruz, after taking those places. The advance on the capital ought to be made at the same time, so as to compel Santa Anna to divide his force.

A good deal has been said about the extension of slavery beyond the Rio Grande. My design in these letters is simply to state facts and give honest opinions. I am not an abolitionist, nor inter-ested in the question of slavery, nor will I suffer my party feel-ings to bias my judgment in relation to Mr. Polk and the democratic administration. The idea of negro slavery beyond the Rio Grande, is, in my opinion, erroneous. The climate is doubtless, adapted to the culture of sugar and cotton ; but then negro slaves cannot be retained on the Mexican frontier longer than they shall think proper to remain in slavery. They would escape into Mexican territory when they pleased ; and there being but few negroes in that country, and none having been held in slavery, they would enjoy a consideration there, un-known even in the free States of the Union. The wealthy Mexicans would not want their services, as they have already a cheaper kind of servitude in their peons, or half indian laborers. Negro slavery was once attempted to be introduced into Mexi-co for the culture and manufacture of the sugar cane, but failed, and the slaves set free. The peons, with a nominal free-dom, are actually slaves. They receive trifling wages, scarcely sufficient to provide them with the bare necessaries of life. It is even doubtful, whether a slave population can be placed nearer than the Nueces, on account of their facilities for escape.

A large proportion of Southern Texas presents the same objection to the removal of the Southern planter. These Mexican acquisitions, or proposed acquisitions, are greatly overrated in the slave holding States, and the danger is equally magnified in the minds of those who are opposed to the further extension of slavery. Neither of these parties are disposed to view the subject in a practical light; it is like the dispute in the fable about the color of the Camelion—one asserted that it was black, and the other that it was white, but when exposed to view, it proved to be green!

LETTER 4.

Victory of Monterey.—The prospects of peace.

SEPTEMBER, 1846.

SIR : Another glorious victory has been achieved by our gallant army! I begin to think that there is scarcely any thing impossible for such men, with such leaders as Taylor and Worth. The incidents of the taking of Monterey would afford materials not merely for a chapter, but a volume.

Surely Mexico will now embrace our offer of peace. The inability of the Mexicans to cope with us is now placed beyond a doubt. We have beaten them in the field two to one, they attacking us; and we have taken one of their strongest cities in spite of fortifications and barricades, and superior numbers. The magnanimity and generosity of the conquerors surely must have some effect on them, unless they are absolutely mad.

The distance of our army from Saltillo is about eighty miles, the way lying through mountain gorges and narrow defiles capable of complete defence in the hands of a brave and determined people. It seems there is something wanting in these people, which puzzles me. It must be, either want of skill and courage in the officers, or a want of patriotism and bravery in the soldiery and inhabitants.

Saltillo may be regarded as the pass of the Sierra Madre, rather than Monterey ; because, from Saltillo there is a road to Presidio on the Rio Grande, and thence to San Antonio of Texas. There should be another division, or rather army, to take this road, and form a junction with General Taylor at Saltillo. Perhaps, that under General Wool, instead of proceding to Chewawa, may take that course.* The range of mountains called the Sierra Madre, forms an impenetrable barrier between the States west of the Rio Grande and the other Mexican States. There are said to be but three passes : the first, from Tampico, by following the Panuco river from the head of its navigation, but affording only a mule track ; the second, that of Saltillo ; and the third, by the Rio Conchas to Chewawa. The distance from Saltillo to Tampico, is not less than six hundred miles ; and after ascending the mountains to the table land, there is nothing but a dreary desert for at least three hundred miles. This, at once suggests the difficulty of the march to Mexico ; and, also, the difficulty on the part of Mexico of sending armies to recover the country between the mountains and the Rio Grande. If the war should continue, which I hope may not be the case, these, and other passes (for I have no doubt there are others) should be seized and fortified, instead of making the Rio Grande the line of defence ; establishing fifty assailable points, instead of three, for an enemy's concentrated force to strike wherever that enemy may choose. If conquest be intended, or result from the war, this line of defence along the Sierra Madre would be absolutely necessary to the planting States, as slavery could not be maintained with the Rio Grande as the boundary. In my opinion, the only real advantage which will be gained by this extension of our terri-

* General Wool marched from Paras to Saltillo.

tory, will be the navigation of the Rio Grande, which will open a trade with the Internal Provinces capable of vast extension. Few southern planters would run the risk of taking their slaves west of the Rio Grande, even with the Sierra Madre as the boundary. They would, of course, migrate in single families, and their negroes could escape, if they thought proper, as fast as they came. I have no doubt, many of them would remain of choice, with their owners; but they would be insecure as property, and that would discourage the importation. The navigation of the Rio Grande is capable of great improvement, and it is ascertained that there is an abundance of coal on its banks. These banks will, some day, be crowded with towns and cities, and their fertile soil will support as large a population as the Nile.

There are but two roads by which the city of Mexico can be approached by our invading armies. The first is, from Saltillo, through the populous States of Zacatecas, Guwadelahara, Guanahwato, San Louis, and Queretaro, containing near four millions. Now, is it probable, that these States will offer no resistance to the long march of General Taylor at the head of a handful of men? I do not doubt, but that in the open field, at the head of ten thousand men, he would beat three times that number; but the heavy loss sustained at Monterey must satisfy us that such victories will be dearly bought. It cannot be said that the Mexican soldiers have not fought, and on some occasions, have not fought well, and they may learn to fight better. But let us consider again, what an immense commissariat must accompany an army on such a march, to afford the necessary supplies. Those who are urging the march of General Taylor on Mexico, are, perhaps, not as well acquainted as he is with what is necessary for such an undertaking. The second road is from Vera Cruz, the distance of three hundred miles, through a thickly settled country, but with numerous defiles, and where there must be fighting at every step. Vera Cruz may be taken, and will be taken, and then the Castle will fall. Here will be a depot to supply the invading army as it shall advance, step by step; and is it likely we can land an invading army of sufficient strength to crush the forces of the Republic under Santa Anna? If the Mexicans make but an indifferent use of the means in their power, it would seem to me impossible for us to reach their capital! The province of Mexico alone, not as large as one of our counties, contains a million and a half of people. If they are like our countrymen, I should say it would be impossible for an invading army of thirty thousand men to penetrate three hundred miles through a country so well fortified by nature. We must expect to fight our way through fifty thousand men at least, which Santa Anna could bring into the field. The country is now united against us, under his sway, by every consideration of hatred and religious feeling, if not of patriotism. I consider it madness to undertake such a march with twenty thousand men, regulars and volunteers, however chivalrous they may be, if Santa Anna should throw himself between Vera Cruz and Mexico, with [the army he has been collecting and training, with so much industry at San Louis Potosi.

We may hold the other side of the Rio Grande; and as soon as our people crowd into it, and bear some proportion to the population already there, it may be regarded as conquered. As to California, it is already ours, and we must soon be complete masters of it, for it will be occupied by our people. The Texan side of the Rio Grande will be ours in consequence of the towns, garrisons, and settlements which will be rapidly established there. We may take Tampico, and hold it; and we may also take Vera Cruz, and retain it until Mexico comes to terms; and it seems to me impossible that she will not do this in order to regain her only seaport, while we, at the same time, cut off all her foreign trade! Nothing but the most stupid, blind, and ignorant obstinacy would prevent her from treating with us under such circumstances. I approve the taking California, and New Mexico, for the purpose of holding them under sequestration, until Mexico shall be willing to make peace on just and reasonable terms. Since the armistice, on the surrender of Monterey, two months must elapse before any further steps can be taken by General Taylor. He was in no condition to advance further than Saltillo, at any rate ; and, perhaps, without completing his conquests of the country east of him, towards the gulf, it would have been un-wise to have moved beyond Monterey. He had important preparations to make, of a very different character from those of his forced march on that city. And, besides, he entertained hopes, as we all did, that during the breathing spell, some means might be found to put an end to the war. In the capitulation of Monterey, he has shown himself as humane as he is brave.

Letter 5.

Capitulation of Monterey—Ideas of conquests in Mexico.

October 26, 184

Sir : When I wrote my last letter I had not seen the capitu-lation of Monterey, at least the official report. It appears, that the terms were conditional, and allow no more time than is ab-solutely requisite for Gen. Taylor to make his arrangements for ulterior movements. The city was taken by a forced march, with only a part of the troops. The attempt to cast censure, by indirection, on this meritorious officer, betrays a jealousy of his growing popularity. The capture of Monterey is of im-mense importance, as well on account of its being one of the keys of Mexico; as on account of the vast amount of public property, in arms and munitions captured, which Mexico is in no condition to replace. That city was a strong hold under the Spaniards before the Mexican revolution, and contained a great quantity of cannon, transported with immense difficulty and expence, from the city of Mexico. It was in fact, the metropolis of the provinces of the Rio Grande; and if a new confederacy should be formed by those States, it would be the seat of the federal Government. In a few weeks, the sickly season will be over; the surviving sick will be again fit for duty, the commissariat will be enabled to complete its supplies, and transportation for the army, considerable reinforcements will reach the seat of war, and then we may expect an onward movement.

General Taylor having now gained a safe footing, must go to work to consolidate his occupation, or if you will, his conquest of the country between the Rio Grande, the mountains, and the Gulf. This extensive tract of country, as large as Italy, and resembling it in scenery, climate, and soil, is now cut off by our arms and by its natural boundary, from the rest of Mexico. It ought to be completely occupied, by fortifying the principal points on the Rio Grande, the mountain passes of the Sierra Madre, and also by the occupation of the chief towns of New Leon, Caawilla, and Tamaulipas. Tampico, of course, must be taken by a combined land and naval attack. It has a shallow sea coast from Tampico to the mouth of the Rio Grande, of four hundred miles, whilst it stretches east and west, between the mountains and the river, nearly double that distance. Here is an extent of surface equal to that from the Potomac to the Savannah and east of the Appalachian chain. It is capable of containing four millions of souls, and in the hands of Americans, would be rapidly filled up by them and European emigrants. The climate is said to be delightful, and much more temperate than might be expected from its latitude. I have rated its population at five hundred thousand; this estimate may be too high; but it is possible, that the common estimate may be too low. The following is that given by a recent pamphlet, including Chewawa:

New Leon,	- - 100,000	Monterey,	- - 15,000
Tamaulipas,	- 150,000	Tampico,	- - 6,000
Coawilla,	- - 125,000	Monclova,	- - 3,000
Chewawa,	- - 112,000	Chewawa,	- - 30,000

487,000

This population, it is true, is scattered over a very large space, and more occupied in pastoral, than in agricultural pursuits, with little trade or manufactures. Their flocks of sheep and horned cattle, are immense, while they raise vast numbers of horses and mules. Being shut out from all communication with the Southern provinces, they can be conquered by our arms, and made to stay conquered, by the American emigrants who will immediately pour into every habitable district. A small, well appointed regular army of five thousand men, with an equal number of volunteers, replacing each other at intervals, will be sufficient for the purpose.

The occupation of this important country, should be complete before attempting any thing further. By grasping at too much, we may fail to realize any thing. If our object be *conquest*, it will be one of the greatest (even thus circumscribed) ever effected by the same numerical force. After consolidating this splendid acquisition, instead of marching on the city of Mexico I would take the course to Durango, and thence to Mazatlan on the Pacific, thus cutting off one half of the mine district, and giving us a direct communication with that ocean, of such immence importance to us in a commercial as well as political point of view. If, however, the object be merely to *conquer a peace* with Mexico, the fear of losing at least one half of the territory of the Republic, and the hope of regaining possession of it, would be an inducement to treat, which nothing but the most brutish stupidity can resist. I fear she will persist in the same arrogant folly which induced her to declare, *that she would be satisfied with no boundery short of the Sabine.* She will not consent to receive back her territory by treaty, to the Rio Grand—her wounded pride must be appeased by regaining it by arms—and she will not consent under any circumstances, to yield up California and Santa Fee! We shall be compelled, if she persists in the determination, to hold to the line of the Sierra Madre, and make our boundary from Tampico to Maxatlan. There is no doubt that the administration would now gladly treat for the boundary of the Rio Grand and a portion of Upper California. But if Mexico persists in her obstinacy, we cannot retreat with safety or honor; we may possibly be compelled to adopt the tropic of Cancer, as the line from ocean to ocean, and thus add to our confederacy a region as extensive as Europe.

But will England and France look with indifference on this vast acquisition of territory? And suppose they shall be displeased, what can they allege against us? The necessity of the conquest will have been forced upon us by the refusal of Mexico to treat. It is probable, that to the boundary of the Rio Grand, and to the acquisition of a portion of California, with the barren mountains and plains of New Mexico, they may be, comparatively, indifferent. Not so with respect to the wholesale acquisition just mentioned. But what can they say —what can they do? They must address themselves to Mexico, and compel her to negotiate with us, which she still persists in refusing, except on terms which she knows it is impossible for us to concede. In the meantime, let us not follow the example of our proud and arrogant enemy, and refuse all friendly mediation which may lead to an amicable adjustment on reasonable terms.

If, for the next three months, there should be no treaty of peace with Mexico, I shall begin to fear we have entered upon an experiment which may be attended with momentous consequences. It will be a new and fearful career of conquest. I cannot agree with those who propose a retreat; and I know that the American people will never consent to it! Yet, I am well aware of the danger to our confederacy, from such a conquest as that of all Mexico. We must follow the war wherever it may lead; and if it lead to victory it must end in conquest or a magnanimous peace, when Mexico shall be at our feet.

LETTER 6.

Difficulties of the conquest of Mexico. The acquisition of California.

NOVEMBER 2, 1846.

SIR: The conquest of Mexico is talked of as a thing settled, and yet, how few have examined the nature of the undertaking and the difficulties to be encountered and overcome! To form some idea of these, we must take into consideration the number of the inhabitants and the extent of the country to be conquered. It is true, the warlike character and resources of such a country, may not be in proportion, as is the case with the Chinese, from unwillingness to keep pace with other nations in the arts of peace and war. The Mexicans are not in this condition; they either have adopted or may adopt all the improvements in war, at least, of modern European nations. Their military strength ought to bear some proportion to their numbers and resources. If the Indian population is destitute of patriotism, their religious feelings and the influence of the priesthood, over them, ought, in some measure, to supply the deficiency. Let us now consider, what we may expect to encounter in the invasion of Mexico.

The population is estimated at eight millions; of these, five millions are contained in a comparatively small space, of which the capital is the centre. Four fifths of this number are In-

dian, peasantry.; the others, either of the pure Spanish race or
mixed with the Indian. The whole, Mexican territory is said
to be a million and a half of square miles—the whole of the
portion containing the five millions does not exceed three hundred
thousand square miles. The two roads, as already mentioned, are
from Saltillo and from Vera Cruz. Let us see what States and
population General Taylor would have to pass through, and
then we may form some idea of the kind of resistance he may
meet, if any defence at all be attempted :

States.		Chief Cities.	
Zacatecas, -	- 272,000	Zacatecas, -	- 40,000
Guanawhato,	- 500,000	Guanawhato, -	- 60,000
San Louis, -	- 250,000	San Louis, -	- 25,000
Queretaro, -	- 200,000	Queretaro, -	- 30,000
Guadelahara,	- 800,000	Guadelahara, -	- 90,000
Mexico, -	1,500,000	Mexico, - -	200,000
	3,522,000		

All the above States must be traversed or passed through—
they must be occupied in such a manner as to keep open the
line of march of the army. We must not think that our
marches will be similar to an insurrectionary movement among
themselves. A Mexican General, at the head of a column, ap-
proaches the city of Mexico, or Guadelahara, a *pronunciamento*
takes place among the soldiers and citizens, and they invite the
insurgent army to enter as friends and countrymen. If we
look for such *pronunciamentos* in favor of an American invading
army, especially of heretics, we will be disappointed. There
was nothing of this at Monterey, and the further we penetrate
to the interior, the less there will be of this kind of faterniza-
tion.

But did not Cortez take the city of Mexico with only nine
hundred men ? Not exactly ; Cortez had, as his allies, two
hundred thousand Indian warriors, twenty thousand of whom
were Tlascalans, the bravest of that region. The taking the

city occupied seventy days, after a terrific slaughter. He divided his army into four divisions, of fifty thousand each, entering the city at different points, and leveling the houses in the way, until the different armies met in the great square. Even if the Mexican armies should avoid pitched battles, they can fortify strong natural positions, and being well provided with artillery, and having good engineers, it would be strange if they did not avail themselves of these advantages. We must expect hard fighting in the mountain passes which abound, and also in taking towns entirely constructed of brick or stone, and incombustible. General Whitlock attempted to take the city of Buenos Ayres, which had little or no defence, except the barricades across the streets and the flat roofs of the houses; his army was twelve thousand strong, and was repulsed with great loss. The Texan mode of burrowing through the houses had not then been invented. I do not say, that General Taylor would not be able to reach Mexico, but it would be after very hard fighting.

Let us now consider what is to be overcome on the Vera Cruz line of march.

States.		Chief Cities.	
Mexico,	- - 1,500,000	Mexico,	- - 200,000
*Michuacan,	- 450,000	Valladolid,	- 25,000
*Wahaca,	- - 600,000	Wahaca,	- - 40,000
Puebla	- - 900,000	Puebla,	- - 60,000
Vera Cruz,	- 200,000	Vera Cruz,	- 15,000
Chiapa,	- - 100,000	Chiapa,	- - 3,000
Tobasco	- - 75,000	Tobasco,	- - 5,000
	4,347,000		

The army, by way of Vera Cruz, would have to pass through four millions; and would meet with greater difficulties on the way than that from Saltillo. I am supposing, that while the invading army advances from this latter place, the

* I have endeavored to accommodate the spelling to the pronunciation.

States along the other road will remain passive ; and so of the
army taking its march from Vera Cruz, that the northern
States will not take part. But this will not be the case. It
will, therefore, be necessary to take both roads at once, and
advance with two armies simultaneously, at an enormous expense and loss of life. It is true, we may find efficient allies
in the discords among the Mexicans themselves, which may
prevent them from uniting against us. The Indians may remain perfectly passive ; the men of property, tired of internal
revolutions, and despairing of ever seeing a settled government
in their country, may desire to seek security and peace under
the wings of the American eagle. These dissentions and jea-
lousies, although of a different kind from those which favored
the conquest by Cortez, may lead to the same result. If they
were a patriotic and united people, the attempt to conquer
them would seem to me hopeless. Yet, when we consider the
force they can bring into the field in defence of their homes,
and as they believe, of their altars, instigated by hatred towards
us, and that sense of degradation, which even the dullest of the
human race must feel at the idea of subjugation by a foreign
enemy, we cannot but expect a powerful resistance. They
ought to be able to arm and embody two hundred thousand
men for defence. This is a very different affair from marching
an army a thousand miles to attack Texas. They would be
called out to defend the very soil on which they exist, and it
seems incredible, that they would not respond to the call.

And should we make ourselves masters of the capital, will
this be the conquest of the whole country ? When Cortez
took the city, he, at the same time, overturned the dynasty and
Empire of Montezuma, which had become odious to the sur-
rounding nations. It was, in fact, those nations which over-
threw that empire, under the guidance and with the aid of the
Spaniards, little thinking, that they were only fighting for a
change of masters. And suppose, that notwithstanding our
signal success in taking the Metropolis, the Mexican Congress

retiring to some other city should still persist in refusing to make peace on our terms, or on any terms, what are we then to do? We must go on to conquer, and hold each seperate State, or we must retire, without either conquering the country or conquering a peace. We should bring back laurels and glory, but foiled and baffled in the objects for which we made such mighty efforts. And I confess, I should be sorry to annex such a population, incapable of defending themselves, incapable of self government, and who must be our dependants. or rather bondsmen. The conquests and annexation of nations on the soil of Italy, gave strength to Rome, but when she acquired distant provinces as dependencies, and established colonies, the government became hopelessly corrupt, and the empire fell by its own weight. It is not so much the annexation of territory, as of people unfitted for republican government, that I dread. If it be necessary to govern them as dependencies, a degree of corruption will be so rapidly introduced into our Government, that its whole character will be changed, and republican virtue will hardly be a name among us.

These, after all, are but speculations, and may prove to be visionary. Our scope of vision into the future is very limited. The great event of the war, in my estimation, is the taking of California. As respects Mexico, it was a mere waif or derelict, liable to be seized by the first comer; and, in fact, we were only about a week before the British squadron, who were utterly astonished to see our flag flying at Monterey and San Francisco, when it was their design to place St. George's cross there. It was merely a question as to who should occupy the country, and surely, in such an alternative, no American can hesitate to say, that possession should be taken by us. It was lost to Mexico, at any rate; and, in the hands of Great Britain, would have been an endless source of vexation to us, and, perhaps, lead to ultimate rupture with that country. We have now a sea coast on the Pacific corresponding to that on the Atlantic.

Our republic stretches from sea to sea, and in time, a land communication will be established between the two, reducing the distance more and more every day. The Republic thus fronts Europe on the east, and Asia on the west, with an ocean boundary, beyond which we cannot go. Here let our proud progress be stayed! Let us be content with filling up the vast space, and improving our condition and the condition of our fellow men. An immense commerce must spring up in less than half a century, from our Pacific coast, with the five hundred millions of people, who inhabit the shores washed by the western and Indian oceans!

LETTER 7.

The War will make us better acquainted with each other.

DECEMBER 5, 1846.

There is one advantage we shall derive from the war: we shall become better acquainted with our southern neighbor, and she will become better acquainted with us. Even in a geographical point of view, in spite of all the writers, from Humboldt down to the latest, and in spite of all the map makers, the American public, is very imperfectly acquainted with Mexico. In nothing is this more remarkable than in the extent of surface, distance of places, and in the amount of population, of which we have no adequate conception. The ignorance of the Mexicans respecting the United States is, of course, still greater. When Santa Anna invaded Texas he actually spoke of marching to Washington in case our Government interfered! We have very little idea of the distance from the Rio Grande to the capital of Mexico; but the thousands who have marched over it in various directions, and the numerous publications giving accounts of military expeditions, will render the country more familiar to our people than it could be in the usual course of things, in fifty years.

In our imaginations, it has been a region of romance, associated with gold and silver, with a climate and beauty of an earthly paradise. Our soldiers and volunteers will return with very different impressions ; taken as a whole, it is vastly inferior to the United States, in natural wealth, in fertility of soil, in climate, and in every thing calculated to minister to human happiness. That incessant craving for the delights of the land of Montezuma, will be effectually cured, and with it, that wild spirit of conquest, which has prevailed until now, in the southern and western portions of the confederacy. It will be effectually cured, and nothing else would have cured it. We shall rest satisfied that our own is, incomparably, a finer country, and, in fact, one of the most favored portions of the Globe. We have no *tierras calientes*, where the vegetable growth is, indeed, most luxuriant, but man looses all his energy, and becomes little better than a vegetable. Their *tierras templadas*, or temperate lands, in general, are barren rocks or dry plains, which cannot be cultivated without irrigation. And when we look at the population, their want of well ordered government, the barbarous ignorance and indolence of the masses, their religious, or rather superstitious bigotry, their robberies and assassinations in cold blood, where is the American who would not prefer his own country ? We have, no doubt, many things among us to deplore and to amend ; but what are these in comparison to the state of things continually presented in those countries which are said to be " blessed of God and cursed of man ?" I do not assent to the first part of this expression, for, I believe, there is no portion of the earth, of the same extent, " so blessed of God," as these United States.

In one thing we have been undeceived ; we supposed that the Mexicans are a rich people, that is, possessed abundant stores of the necessaries and luxuries of life. So far from it, that we have been compelled to draw nearly all of our supplies for our armies from the States. There are, doubtless, rich individuals among them, but the mass of the people are miserably poor. They lay up no stores, and have little beyond what is required by their immediate wants. The very abundance of the productions of nature may be one of the causes of this general poverty. As a people, they are sunk in sloth, in vice and ignorance. I speak in general, for there are, no doubt, numerous exceptions. Their opinions of the "Yankees," as they call us, in contempt and derision, is likely to undergo an entire change. They will entertain a different opinion of us; they will look upon us with fear and respect, and will be as anxious to cultivate a good understanding as they were to insult us and ill treat our citizens. Hereafter, their Government will take a second thought before it countenances the plunder and murder of Americans. Treaties of peace will be respected, and we may venture into the country without danger to person or property, provided we conduct ourselves with propriety.

There are many of the geographical features of so vast a country, especially as to its mountains, table lands, and rivers, differing entirely from our portion of the continent. For instance, the character of the table lands beyond Monterey would not be understood without the explanation, that the Mexican mountains are not in regular ranges or ridges like the Alleghanies, with intervening valleys, but present, on the eastern side, the appearance of giant ramparts of naked rock, through which fissures have been made by torrents; while on their summit, a vast plain, six or seven thousand feet above the sea, like a table raised above the floor, stretches out for hundreds of miles, with occasional depressions and peaks piled up to the height of five or six thousand feet more, and covered with perpetual snow. We have no such mountains. The sides of our mountains are nearly all fertile, at least, east of the Mississippi. The precipitous sides of the *Sierra Madre* are broken through by several rivers, which, in the course of a hundred miles, descend six or seven thousand feet, and in consequence of this, excepting a short distance from their mouths in the Gulf of Mexico, are not fit for navigation. It is along the courses of these rivers, that the passes are found: such as that of the Panuco from Tampico; that of the Tula, near Victoria; that of the San Juan, from Monterey to Saltillo, and the Conchas, towards Chewawa. The want of good roads from the interior, and good harbors on the Gulf, essentially render the eastern portion of Mexico, an inland country. The Alvarado, Guasacualco, and Tobasco, are almost the only exceptions. The States north and east of the Sierra Madre, comprising those which we now hold, although not yet completely subdued, have no water transportation to the coast, excepting by means of the Rio Grande. The want of a carriage road is exemplified by the fact, that the British company engaged in working the mines of Catorce, which are not more than three hundred miles in a direct line from Tampico, having landed their engines at that place, could not transport them direct to San Luis, but were obliged to go north towards Matamoras, and then take the direction of Monterey and Saltillo. From the latter place, after ascending to the table land, they proceed to San Louis, making a circuit of more than twelve hundred miles, and which consumed four months.

The delightful country which I have described, as the States of New Leon, Coawilla, and Tamaulipas, is equal in extent to the eastern parts of Virginia and North and South Carolina, and large enough for a kingdom. It is, in general a plain, but not flat; on the contrary, picturesque, with a fine soil, admirably adapted to all the productions of the temperate climates, but free from frosts.. This country we shall be compelled to hold, even if our conquests should extend no further. We cannot abandon it *without a treaty of peace and boundaries*, and to which, from present appearances, Mexico will not agree. We shall not give it up unless for a complete cession of California and New Mexico, with the boundary of the Rio Grande. The population of those States is, now, perhaps, equal to that of our Southern States during our revolutionary war, and would easily contain four or five millions. For defence, it ought now to bring fifteen or twenty thousand fighting men into the field, in guerrilla parties, and poorly armed. If supported by some regular troops, the rancheros might give us trouble. But cut off from all supplies, with no rallying points or fortified places, we could by pushingt he war vigorously, effectually subdue them. If we fall back on the Rio Grande, we leave the whole country west of it, open to the operations of Santa Anna; and we shall be compelled to establish a chain of fortifications along the great river, for at least two thousand miles. On the other hand, the table land of the Sierra Madre, and on the west, towards the Pacific, being only accessible by a few passes, the inhabitants once completely subdued, must remain so. That mountain boundary is, infinitely, more easy to defend, than the line of the river; a river, which would be bordered in its whole length by an enemy, who might send detachments at any moment to make destructive inroads. It would be necessary to have both sides of the river, without which, it would be a bad boundary. If we confine ourselves to the east side of it, the inhabitants on the other bank, in case of hostilities, can at any time call in the aid of the Mexican Government. Collisions will be unavoidable, and Texas will be continually threatened, unless we keep up, at great expense, a permanent force along the line. But taking the mountains as the boundary, we could keep Mexico in her shell, until the valley shall be filled by American and European population. There is, no doubt, unappropriated land; but, even supposing the whole to be claimed under grants to the church, and to individuals, these might justly be subjected to forfeitures and confiscations, partial or total, in case of refusal to own allegiance. The tenures of all these lands are, in their nature, feudal; that is, the fee is in the sovereign, whoever that may be, and subject to be resumed and regranted at the pleasure of the sovereign. The tenure or holding, is not allodial as with us; it is rather political or military, if I may so express myself, than legal.* This subject is not generally understood among us, and it would occupy too much space to explain it more fully. If Mexico compels us to conquer the country described, we must annex it, but cannot do this without republicanizing it first; and this, again, cannot be done without abolishing the feudal system, and changing the tenure of the lands. Still, I am no advocate of conquest; I would rather take the boundary of the Rio Grande by fair treaty, than hold the States bordering on that river, by the rights of war, which are regarded by all barbarous nations, and by Mexico herself, is the highest, and most glorious of all titles.

The policy of Santa Anna, at present, is to act on the defensive, preparatory to taking the offensive. He is now at work at San Luis, in collecting and organizing a powerful army, the most formidable ever yet seen in the republic. He will address himself to the Mexicans, with such appeals as may rouse them to a sense of their danger, and will, perhaps, attempt to lay hold of the immense riches of the church, to sustain the national cause. In the latter, he will probally fail; it is the greater power in Mexico, for power does not centre exclusively in the army, and but a small portion of it in the people, if there can be said to be a people at all. His object is, no doubt, to make himself a *dictator*, or an absolute despot; and this he cannot accomplish, without, in the first instance, having the support of the church. When sufficiently strong by means of the army, he can then use the church as a part of his machinery. Every thing depends on his success in this war. If he succeeds in repelling the invasion, he will, in all probability, be able to establish his power on a permanent footing of hereditary despo-

---

* I speak of the large grants, the smaller are allodial, as also, the grants on condition of settlement.

tism. To conquer the country, our shortest course is, to deal at once with the church and the great land holders, and make them responsible for their peons; for the proprietors not only own the land, with but few exceptions, but also own the population, just as the Russian noble owns the serfs of his estate.

Since the Mexican revolution, the States and territories north and west of the line from Tampico to Mazatlan, and even the States which I have mentioned, directly west of the great river, have been rapidly returning to their original state of barbarism. Contrary to the usual course of things on this continent, the indian tribes have here been, for years, encroaching on the whites, instead of being encroached upon and driven back. In the States of Durango, Chewawa, Sonora, Sinaloa, and in Lower California, the Apaches and Camanches, are continually laying waste, robbing, plundering, and murdering, and each succeeding year, their ravages are becoming more and more extensive. Under the royal government, posts were established every where, troops were kept up, and the inhabitants protected, by pursuing the marauding parties, the only way in which a country can be protected from savages. But they did not arm the inhabitants, and require them to assist in defending themselves. There was no militia, and consequently, when left to themselves, they are perfectly helpless. There could be no greater blessing to them, than to be placed under the protection of the United States. I repeat, that my object is not to encourage a spirit of conquest. In indulging in these speculations, I endeavor to be guided by the spirit of truth.

LETTER 8.

Slight hopes of peace—State of the war—The situation of General Taylor.

JANUARY, 1847.

SIR: When Santa Anna declares, that there can be no negotiations for peace until the *national* territory shall have been evacuated by the troops of the United States, he means by the *national* territory, from the Rio Grande to the Sabine, as well as those portions of Mexico, which we now hold by invasion. Not a single official declaration on the part of the Mexican Government can be produced, in which any other boundary than the Sabine is even supposed. In the last proclamation of Almonte, this is the only boundary acknowledged by him. As long as this is maintained by Mexico, peace is impossible. The Rio Grande was the boundary of the Province of Texas, under the Spanish Government, and as such, was claimed, both by France and the United States, as part of Louisiana, under the treaty of Ildelonso, when ceded by Spain. It is the boundary claimed by Texas after her separation from Tamaulipas and Coawilla, with which Texas had, for a time, been united, to form a State of the Mexican confederacy ; and on separating from that confederacy, she returned to the ancient limits. It is this ancient Texas we claim, and not the Texas arranged in connection with Tamaulipas and Coawilla. But Santa Anna and Almonte now acknowledge no boundary but the Sabine, notwithstanding their treaty with Texas, expressly establishing the Rio Grande.

Persons not reflecting on our present position, as respects our enemy, exclaim, " let us make peace—let us put an end to this unfortunate war". This supposes, that it is *in our power* at any moment, to make peace, when, from the very declarations of Mexico, she is unwilling to treat with us, unless we first acknowledge ourselves vanquished, and agree to retire, yielding every thing we have been contending for ! ONE may make war, but it takes TWO or more, to make peace. We may, indeed, fall back on the Rio Grande, and then to the Sabine, thus exposing ourselves to the contempt and derision of the world ; and there are well meaning people, who propose this course. But, judging from a knowledge of human nature, it is not difficult to perceive, that the great majority of the people of

6

the United States will never consent to such a degrading submission, even if it were prudent, as a mere matter of interest, which it is plainly not, however it may be recommended by abstract considerations of moral or religious duty, or rather of sickly sentimentality.

Let us consider what are the steps to be taken to bring about negotiations for peace. The olive branch ought to be continually held out to the enemy; and our agents should not be prevented by pride or offended dignity, from renewing at every moment, the offer to treat. It would be magnanimous on our part, and also continue us in the right. Suppose the proposition come from Mexico, what will it be, and how made? It is not probable that commissioners will be sent direct to Washington, or invited from us, to Mexico. A communication may be addressed to our Governmet declaring a willingness to treat, in all probability, clogged with conditions of the withdrawal of our naval and military forces, and proposing an armistice pending negotiations. To the latter, we cannot accede, without giving decided advantage to the enemy. The evacuation of the country we now hold would not be listened to for a moment; it would at once be yielding all the advantages we have gained at so much cost, as the *means of coercing Mexico to treat of peace.* The attempt at negotiation may thus fail at various stages, and it may fail entirely; at all events, there will be unavoidable delay. There is nothing before us, at present, but as a vigorous prosecution of the war, *and at the same time, preparations on a much larger scale than we have hitherto made.*

What is the state of the war at this moment? We have made wonderful progress, if not towards conquest, at least, towards bringing the enemy to terms. But we are obliged to keep up three very extensive lines, without speaking of California and New Mexico. The first, is along the Rio Grande, rom Presidio to Matamoras, of seven hundred miles; the next, that from Comargo to Monterey ; and the third, from Tampico to the same place, a distance of nearly six hundred. It is absolutely necessary to keep up the two first, in order to furnish supplies for our troops in all their operations; although, since the occupation of Tampico, a portion of these may be obtained from that quarter. But, between the mountains and the river, there is an enemy's country, which, although thinly inhabited, is capable of interrupting our communications by their rancheros aided by Mexican troops, and led by Mexican officers, even i they cannot bring a sufficient force at any point, to meet ours in the field. We hear of large bodies of irregular cavalry, which may prove formidable in case the war be prolonged. This kind of force, thus far, appears to have been much overated, but it may take lessons from us, and improve. Their horses, although small, may be better trained, and their riders, equal to any in the world, may be provided with better arms— the sabre, and pistol, and carbine, instead of the lance and lasso.

It was supposed that there were but two passes through the mountains to the table land ; but a third, that of Tula, near Victoria, is now spoken of. This river, appears to penetrate the great barrier between Tampico and Monterey, and takes its rise in the table land, between San Luis, and Zacatecas. It is possible, that the army of Santa Anna may, by this route, keep open a communication with the valley of the Rio Grande, and even send large reinforcements of cavalry and infantry through this pass, so as to threaten our lines on the Rio Grande and Tampico. According to the last accounts, our troops were marching towards Victoria. I should think it all important to take possession of that pass, and close it completely.

There are still paragraphs in the papers, speaking of the intended march from Monterey, or Tampico, to San Luis. I think this highly improbable. It will be unsafe for us to move until we are completely masters of the whole country between the river and the mountains, and of all the passes to the table land. It would not do to leave this country in our rear, with all our military depots, but weakly guarded. Of one thing I will speak with confidence ; that we shall need all the troops we have on the present scene of operations, and all we shall be able to send for some time. The descent on Vera Cruz, which is said to be in preparation, under the immediate direction of the commander in chief, General Scott, will require, at least, twenty thousand men, and if any considerable proportion be withdrawn from General Taylor, it will leave him in a very perilous situation. What is to prevent Santa Anna from making his head quarters at Victoria ? It is said, that cannon cannot be transported by the Tula pass. This may, or may not be. Things deemed impossible have been accomplished by men of bold and enterprizing spirit, as he is said to be. Napoleon crossed the Alps in spite of impossibilities, and appeared suddenly in the plains of Lombardy ; and I should think the difficulties a hundred times greater than would be encountered by the Mexican Napoleon. I confess, I entertain serious apprehensions for our troops, although of the best materials, and admirably commanded.

Santa Anna has, at this moment, a great advantage ; he is posted at San Luis with an army of twenty five or thirty thousand men. Thus concentrated at one point, he will be enable to strike, with his whole force, or the greater part of it, at Tampico, Saltillo, or Victoria, while our forces, are necessarily divided into comparatively small bodies. He can act with perfect secrecy, in a friendly country, and with a perfect knowledge of all our movements, while we are ignorant of his. If he should attack us with his whole force at any one point, he may roll back the tide of war, and drive us beyond the Rio Grande. Under present circumstances, instead of weakening our lines, prudence requires that we should strengthen them.

Looking to the hazzards of war, and the *dangers* following

on conquests, the idea has suggested itself, of inviting the
States of the lower Rio Grande to establish a separate confederacy, under our protection ; and if Mexico persists in refusing
to treat, then, to enter into a treaty of peace, alliance, and limits
with this new confederacy, thus indemnifying ourselves for
Mexican spoliations, by taking California and New Mexico,
with the right of way to Mazatlan, and leaving Mexico to re-
pent of her folly at leisure.

LETTER 9.

*Present advantageous position of our army—The necessity
for greater efforts—Our present force insufficiet to march
from Vera Cruz to Mexico.*

FEBRUARY 13TH, 1847.

SIR : The last intelligence from the seat of war has given much
relief to those who were beginning to feel uneasy about the
situation of our troops. Generals Taylor and Patterson have
taken Victoria or New Santander, and the line is therefore established from Saltillo to Tampico. The line of the Sierra
Madre has already been described; it is certainly of a very
peculiar character; it now presents only three points of attack, and that of Saltillo, the only one practicable for wheel
carriages, and consequently, for the advance of an army with
its parks of artillery. It is from this quarter, alone, that General Taylor need fear the march of Santa Anna; but he will
have to cross at least three hundred miles of arid plains ; and
it is said, that the water tanks have been destroyed by his
order, which looks as if he intended to prevent the march of
General Taylor on San Luis, rather than undertake the
march to Saltillo. It, appears, that he has a large force at
Tula, about equi distant from Saltillo and Victoria.

By guarding this line, the valley can be cut off from all supplies from Mexico; with the exception of a small quantity of

indian corn, and the herds of the ranchos, very little can be procured in it for the support of an army. Our own safety requires, that we should take possession of all the principal towns as soon as possible, and garrison them with a sufficient force. It will, also, be necessary to establish civil authority, for the country thus cut off from the central Government. Its head must necessarily be military, as also the local superior authorities, although using the machinery of Alcaldes &c., for the purpose of carrying it on. The political Government, must be suspended, as the consequence of being cut off from both the State and federal authorities of Mexico.

It would now seem to be the general impression, that nothing effectual can be done to bring Mexico to terms without taking Vera Cruz, and marching to the capital ; and this appears to be the opinion of General Taylor at least, that if the march be resolved upon, then Vera Cruz, is the proper point to start from and not from Saltillo. A short time will determine.

We have, thus far, been operating at vast expense with, an army of fifteen thousand men, about one half regulars, and the other half, volunteers, on the remote, thinly inhabited, northern frontier of Mexico ; and we talk of marching through a densly peopled country with numerous defiles ! If there be any thing like the resistance made by us during the revolutionary war, thirty thousand men, at least, will be required for the march from Vera Cruz to Mexico. A part of the force under General Taylor may now be spared, but not so as to weaken and disable him from repelling a part of the army of Santa Anna, if he should think proper to detach it, for the purpose of attacking Saltillo. It would be presumptuous in me to venture an opinion on military movements ; but considering the formidable army now organized by Santa Anna, and the uncertainty as to the point which he means to attack, I should think, that it would not be safe to draw off any very considerable portion of General Taylor's force from the defence of the lines they at present occupy.

It is in our power to seize all her ports, and cut off all the trade of Mexico; and then, holding the lines we now occupy, it will be strange, if she persists in refusing to make peace. The fear of the loss of the interior and northern provinces, and the interuption in her trade, thus shut up in her shell, may have that effect, if any thing can. We have for the present, given stability to her Government by outward pressure. Our only security is to retain the hold we have; and perhaps, it may be necessary to attempt something on a still larger scale; but for this, we are not yet prepared. General Scott may take Vera Cruz, and then block up the road to Mexico, but I have seen no force yet, even on paper, sufficient to undertake the march to that capital. If, by withdrawing a large portion of General Taylor's force, the line he now occupies be too much weakened, Santa Anna, will at once, take advantage of it, and regain the country on that side of the Rio Grande. In doing this, he will compell the army which may be landed at Vera Cruz, to return in all haste to Tampico, or Point Isabel. The crisis is now fast approaching, when it will become a question of national prowess—shall we cry, " hold, enough !" or make a mighty effort to obtain the victory? I wish to see my country do right, and justice to all nations ; at the same time, I should be sorry to see our flag humbled, under any circumstances, and in a war with any nation on the Globe ! I wish to see that flag wave proudly, and respected, wherever it may be carried, not tarnished and humbled, by defeat—insulted, scorned, treated with contempt, instead of affording a shelter and protection to our citizens, wherever they may be. But, firmly convinced, as I am, that our country is in the right, and our enemy in the wrong, I should feel the mortification ten fold, if we failed to obtain a just and honorable peace by the only means left us, *after our enemy has repeatedly spurned the olive branch.*

LETTER 10.

Annexation of Texas—The suspension of diplomatic relations, the immediate causes of the war.

FEBRUARY, 1847.

SIR: In these letters, I have endeavored to repress all party feeling, thinking it a duty, in a contest with a foreign nation, in time of actual war, to take the side of my country, unless so grossly and palpably in the wrong, as to admit of no justification 'or defence. I repeat, that it is my sincere conviction, that justice is on our side, and this after as full, and dispassionate an examination of the subject as I am able to bestow. The contrary, is generally assumed, or taken for granted, by the party to which I belong ; and yet the speech of Mr. Webster, at Philadelphia, which expresses the same opinion, is highly applauded. He condemns the administration of Mr. Polk, (not the cause of the country,) solely on the ground of bringing on a state of actual hostilities, without the previous approbation of Congress, while he admits, that Mexico is in the wrong in the causes which led to it the annexation of Texas. But the act of the President, is a domestic question between him and American people. The causes previously existing, and which would have justified Congress in making war, constitute a different question from that of expediency, or of the distribution of powers, under the Constitution. He concedes, that if the constituted authorities of the Union had thought proper to resort to this course, there was ample cause to justify it. To this, I assent, and will endeavor to give the reasons on which my opinion is founded, according to my view of the subject ; professing, at the same time, a sincere respect for the opinion of those who may differ from me. I admit that the march from the Nueces to the Rio Grande, had the effect of *hastening* hostilities ; but, in my opinion, it did no more than hasten, for the appeal of arms was inevitable on the annexation of Texas, unless Mexico receded entirely from the ground she had taken ; of which, I did not see the slightest probability, unless compelled to do so, by the consequences of war, whether begun by her or by us.

Mexico denounces the war as being aggressive on our part, but in all the official State Papers of the high functionaries of that Republic, (I do not refer to subordinate officers or generals,) in all their manifestoes, that aggression is distinctly declared to be *the annexation of Texas*. It was on this ground, that she put an end to all diplomatic intercourse, after having previously announced that she would consider annexation as equivalent to a declaration of war, on our part. It was on this ground, that she refused to *resume* a diplomatic intercourse, and enter into negotiation for a peaceful adjustment of existing differences, until satisfaction should first be made for the alleged wrong. She has not limited her complaints of alleged aggression to the march of our troops to the Rio Grande ; her complaint is, the being deprived of her province of Texas, which she will never renounce ; and she declares her determination never to listen to overtures of peace, until that province shall be evacuated by us. Has she, on any occasion, shown a willingness to accept any other boundary than the Sabine? I have seen no intimation of this kind, emanating from her President or Congress. The contrary is unchangeably persisted in.*
In fact, it could not occur while she persists in her right to the whole of Texas. The annexation is the *casus belli* on the part of Mexico—the paramount consideration—every thing else, is but incidental, or subordinate. The very idea of fixing any other boundary, would imply a relinquishment of her claim.

Now, that great statesman, Mr. Webster, has proved on various occasions, and especially in his Philadelphia speech,

* There is no distinct assertion of boundary in any of her official papers down to the *war proclamation* of the 23d of April, 1846.

7

that annexation of Texas to the United States was no cause of war, because Texas was as much an independent State as Mexico. The act was no more a cause of war on the part of Mexico, than her annexation to the United States would have been a cause of war on the part of Texas. If Mr. Webster be correct, and I think his argument unanswerable, was Mexico justifiable in the course pursued by her towards us on account of that act? Was she justifiable in withdrawing her minister, and ordering away the minister of the United States? These were very high handed and insulting measures, and attended, necessarily, with the serious consequence of putting an end to all peaceful modes of adjusting differences, and leaving the only alternatives of, submission, or war, on our part. But, under the circumstances in which Mexico was placed towards us, it was an act of gross injustice, as well as insult. *She had a treaty obligation to fulfil, in the payment of several millions, as the indemnity for wrongs done to American citizens, and demands had been made upon her for several millions more, which remained unadjusted.* There was, also, a question of boundary to settle—all these matters must be settled either peaceably, or by war—if peaceably, the continuance, or re-establishment of diplomatic intercourse, was indispensable. Her conduct was like that of the debtor who cuts the acquaintance of his creditor, and thinks by that means, to avoid fulfilling his obligations. Let me ask, what would have been the course pursued, (if placed in our situation,) by England or France, or any other high minded Government? I ask any candid man to say, whether they would have borne it as patiently as we have done? I would ask whether there was as much forbearance shown by us with Louis Philippe, on the subject of the French indemnity, or with England in the Northern boundary, and Oregon question? That nation assumes an awful responsibility, which, like Mexico, puts an end to the peaceable ways of diplomacy, leaving no alternative but horrid war, or base submission. Mexico should have paid her debt before she put an end to peaceful intercourse, and she could not do it without injustice, while there were claims still depending. All arguments drawn from considerations of forbearance, humanity, generosity, expediency, are for ourselves—Mexico is entitled to no part in them. In my estimation, the great *error* of Mexico, if so mild a term can be applied, consists in her having terminated all peaceful modes of settling differences; for, as there is no common arbiter between independent nations, their differences in that case, must be settled by war, or not at all.

I am again sustained, by the opinion of Mr. Webster, in respect of the refusal of Mexico to the re-establishment of diplomatic relations proposed by us; and again, in her refusal to meet the more recent overtures for negotiation. The first improper conduct of Mexico has been greatly aggravated by these acts. It has been urged, that Mexico was willing to receive a *commissioner*, to treat in relation to Texas. It is surprising to me, that any one should not see the folly of this proposition. It was only saying, " as you have wronged us, in the annexation of Texas, we will permit you to offer us suitable reparation, and this must precede all other matters between us." The ignorance and presumption of such an idea, is truly Mexican. *If they were sincere in their desire to discuss the subject, what objection could there be to receiving an ambassador, clothed with full powers to settle all matters in dispute?

* Mr. Gallatin makes a strange mistake, when he says, that the refusal, was to receiving a *resident minister*. The refusal was on account of his not being a mere Commissioner on the *single subject of Texas!* What reasonable objection could there be to a resident minister, after a treaty of peace? And if no such treaty were made, then the minister clothed with those powers would take his *departure*, as a matter of course. Mr. Gallatin speaks very *lightly* of a *suspension* of diplomatic intercourse! I regard this, under the circumstance, as most serious. But there was more than suspension; Mexico declared *all negotiations* at an end, and war was, therefore, the only alternative.

What right had Mexico to require us to *admit*, that anexation was an aggression on her rights? There was no proposition to discuss the question of *boundary*, as is frequently asserted, which would be inconsistent with her pretensions. But even that could be more fully settled by one having full authority, than by a mere special commissioner, with limited powers. The whole was but a diplomatic quibble—a deceitful evasion. In the opinion of Mr. Webster, Mexico was wrong in putting an end to diplomatic relations; she was wrong in rejecting our minister under a frivolous pretext, and she continues in the wrong in rejecting overtures of peace, after the commencement of hostilities. Here was a direct advance on our part, superceding the necessity of mediation, a measure only adopted to save the pride of either party, in being the *first* to propose a peace. In all this, Mexico is in the wrong; and here is the whole question, as between her and the United States. The degree of forbearance to be shown, is a question for ourselves alone. The first blow was struck by Mexico, unless the provocation of our march to the Rio Grande, *be considered the first blow.* There is nothing left for us, but to prosecute the war until Mexico shall be willing to enter into peaceable negotiation. Some appear to think that she would be most likely to re-establish diplomatic relations, by our withdrawing our fleets and armies. But this would only be an experiment, and might fail; and if it should fail, our work would have to begin again. This was done when Mr. Slidell landed at Vera Cruz, but without success. Can we place sufficient confidence in Mexico, even after the most positive and dictinct assurances, and still less without any such assurances? For my part, I have no confidence either in the good faith of her present rulers, or in the stability of her Government. What, then, is to be done? I see no way but to retain the advantages we already possess, and to prosecute the war on her territory, as other wars, under like circumstances, would be prosecuted by other nations. What is there to prevent her from entering into negotiations at once ? Pride —folly—but we were not too proud to negotiate with England' at the moment when the war was hottest. At the very moment of signing the treaty of Ghent, the British Commissioner supposed, and ours also, that the British troops were in possession of Louisiana, and one of them observed to the American Commissioner. "You have reason to be satisfied, for you have now regained New Orleans." The idea of falling back on the Rio Grande, in the visionary hope of coaxing Mexico to make peace, and then in case of her refusal, retaking Monterey and Tampico, and the valley of the Rio Grande, would be like the fisherman, who after having one good haul, throws back the best fish into the sea, for the pleasure of retaking them!

———

LETTER 11.

The causes of the war.—The complaints on either side.

FEBRUARY, 1847.

SIR : The tendency of public opinion throughout the civilized world, and especially in the United States, against all wars, may be justly set down as an evidence of the progress of civilization. There are many who regard all wars, defensive as well as offensive, as wicked and inexcusable. Others, justify defensive wars only, as if it were possible for one to defend himself by merely warding off the blows of the assailant. Some regard wars made for conquest merely, as unlawful, and no sound moralist can approve of a war instigated by a motive so unjust and dishonest. But when war is once begun, it unavoidably becomes offensive, as well as defensive, in order to bring the opposite party to terms—it necessarily becomes a war of conquest by holding the enemy's territory as a lawful acquisition, until restored by treaty of peace, if restored at all. No one nation has yet abandoned the practice of war, and I cannot well understand how it can do so, while it is continued by others. In the present unregenerated state of the world, wars are therefore regarded by practical men, as sometimes unavoidable, and even necessary and just. It was the opinion of Washington, that the best security for peace, is in being well prepared for war; and it may be added, to impress other nations with respect or fear of our military prowess. I am convinced, that our last three years war with Great Britain, ensured us a long peace, not only with that power, but with others. I am equally certain, that but for our seven years of revolutionary war, we should have been neither a free nor an independent nation—our magnificent country would not have been " the land of the free, and the home of the brave. " If all wars are " murders and robberies, " as some philanthropists contend, there must be a revolution in our sentiments towards Washington and his brave companions in arms, who offered up their lives for the blessings of freedom and self-government, and of peace, which we have enjoyed.

But I am free to admit, that a civilized nation cannot, without just reproach, engage in a war that is unjust, and that is not, in a certain sense, unavoidable. The nation ought to go beyond, rather than fall short of the strict measure of justice, and she ought to exhaust every means of maintaining peace, before resorting to the *ultimate ratio.*

It is my intention in this letter to look into the causes which have led to the war in which we are now engaged with Mexico. I must premise, that we must take the world as we find it, and we must decide according to the ethicks and practice of the most civilized nations, and not according to standards of morality, which, although perfect in themselves, are inapplicable to the present imperfect state of mankind. It is again to be observed, that among nations, there is no common judge, to whom they are willing to submit their differences, and to obey the decision.

Each is the judge in its own case, and if one should be disposed to do even more than justice, the demands of the other may be out of all reason. It is a rare thing in modern times, for two powerful civilized nations to be involved in hostilities, without previous differences, misunderstandings, or mutual aggressions, and without, also, previous unsuccessful attempts to adjust their differences in a peaceful way. Let us first consider the complaints of Mexico.

These consisted, in the first instance, in the aid afforded by citizens of the United States in the struggle of Texas with Mexico for her independence. But this did not begin with that struggle, but with the efforts of Mexico herself to throw off the allegiance of Spain, in which she was so materially aided by the Americans of Texas, and who continued to be invited into that country for the purpose of giving strength to the Mexican cause. Serious offence was given to Spain in consequence of this volunteer aid of our citizens to her revolted provinces, but, certainly, there was no complaint on the part of those provinces. Their situation changed as soon as they won their independence, and when Texas revolted in consequence of alleged oppression, Mexico assumed the position before occupied by Spain, and complained of the aid afforded by citizens of the United States to Texas. Here is, no doubt, the ground of the ill-feeling on the part of Mexico towards us. How far we are responsible for the acts of our citizens, beyond our jurisdiction, is a question which opens a wide field for discussion, and is one which cannot be discussed in these cursory letters. All I shall say, is, that Mexico had the same right to complain that Spain had, and no more and even less, for it was the consequence of her own act, in calling in our countrymen to help her against Spain. I avoid saying any thing here, as to the merits of the quarrel between Texas and Mexico.

In the contest which ensued between these belligerants, Mexico put forth her whole strength—she entered Texas with a powerful army, commanded by her Chief Magistrate in person, who was at the same time her most distinguished military leader— a leader, who had put down the constitution of 1824, and concentrated the whole power of the State in his own person, and in the person of his own military subordinates. The invsaion was followed by the signal defeat at San Jacinto, by General Houston, and a treaty, *acknowledging the independence of Texas, and recognizing the Rio Grande as the Southern boundary.* I do not mean to discuss the diplomatic question involved in this treaty, my object being in this place, merely to state facts.* Subsequently, with the exception of some inroads on either side, the war ceased—the cause of Mexico became hopeless— the independence of Texas was not only recognized by us, but also by other neutral nations. Her inability to re-conquer Texas, was confessed by Mexico herself; she was even willing to acknowledge her independence on the condition that Texas would not unite herself to the United States—condition which no nation in our place would fail to regard as offensive. Next follows the act on our part in which was merged all other offences, and was, before-hand, declared by Mexico, not only as a cause of war, but equivalent to a declaration of war—the annexation of Texas with its consent. The act has been generally condemned by the whig press, and yet, it is sustained by very high authority : Mr. Webster, as Secretary of State, holds this language : "Mexico may have chosen to consider Texas as having been at all times since 1835, and still continuing, a rebellious province, but the world has been obliged to take a different view of the matter. From the time of the battle of San Jacinto to the present moment, Texas has continued to exhibit the same internal signs of national independence as Mexico herself, and with quite as much stability of government." Again he repeats, " since 1837, the United States have regarded Texas as

*The able speech of Mr. Kauffman in Congress on this subject is not easily refuted. As a jurist, I do not hesitate to pronounce the treaty valid.

an independent sovereignty as much as Mexico. " He says further, "the constitution, public treaties, and laws, oblige the President to regard Texas as an independent State, *and its territory no part of the territory of Mexico.*" In a late public speech at Springfield, Mr. Webster uses the following language, "I do not admit that it was a just ground of complaint on the part of Mexico, that the United States annexed Texas to themselves." From my own unassisted reasoning, I had arrived at the same conclusion with Mr. Webster. The ground taken by the great statesman against the war, was not on account of the annexation of Texas, but of the march of Gen. Taylor, by the order, or sanction of Mr. Polk, whose practical result was inevitable, hostilities, which ought not to have been brought on without the express sanction of Congress, and while there was still a possibility of negotiating. The first, is a question between Mr. Polk and his country, with which Mexico has noth-to do; the other, is a mere question of probability, depending on the willingness on our side to negotiate, and the willingness, or the contrary, on the part of Mexico, to meet us. I will add, that the taking of California and New Mexico, are acts arising out of the war, aud not causes leading to it.

Let us now consider the provocations and complaints on our side; these commenced before any of the alleged grievances on the part of Mexico. They may be placed under two heads; first, the refusal to pay American citizens the debts contracted by their government for the means of carrying on their war of independence; and secondly, for outrages committed on the persons of our people while in the pursuit of their lawful business, and for the illegal seizure and confiscation of their property. The second head covers much the largest amount of injuries complained of: they consist of seizure of vessels in port, on false or frivolous pretexts; of goods and merchandise for public use; of forced loans and civil injuries to persons, and wanton confinement to loathsome prisons, where many perished or

8

lost their health. There were beside, anomalous cases, *some of them involving immense losses, breaking up mercantile establishments, producing ruin, and irreparable injury.

We find as early as the first term of Gen. Jackson, the most ruinous complaints on the part of our fellow-citizens of the wrongs inflicted on them by Mexico. They are such, says he, "as cannot be tolerated by any government endued with a just self-respect, with a proper regard for the opinions of other nations, or with enlightened concern for the permanent welfare of those portions of its people who may be interested in foreign commerce." After enumerating the various classes of outrages, he adds, "citizens of the United States have been imprisoned for long periods of time, without being informed of the offences with which they were charged. Others have been murdered and robbed on the high seas by Mexican officers, without any attempt to bring the guilty to justice." In a subsequent message to Congress, he declares, "that such conduct *would justify immediate war, in the eyes of all nations.*" The same language was repeated by the subsequent administration, in still stronger terms. All this was previous to the alleged wrongs on our part, in respect to Texas, and the only excuse was the revolutionary state, and the consequent disorders under which Mexico was then a sufferer; and this plea, untenable as it is, was respected to such a degree, as to amount to a denial of justice to our own citizens. The American sufferings were aggrava-

*Such as that of Aaron Ligett, who introduced steamboats on the Tobasco river, according to a contract with the government; his boats were seized for public use, his merchandize confiscated, and business and credit destroyed. There is the case of Dr. Baldwin, who was induced to establish saw mills, which were seized when they became profitable, and the lands purchased by him confiscated. There is the case of the empressario contracts in Texas, where lands were granted by Mexico, on condition of colonizing, and when the company brought out colonies at great expense, they were forcibly prevented from taking possession—colonists driven off or imprisoned, and the goods and effects of the company seized.

ted by seeing the prompt and decisive measures of the French to redress similar outrages, when Admiral Baudin blew up the castle of San Juan de Ulloa, and compelled the Mexican government to pay a million of dollars on the deck of his vessel. How is it possible, after these facts, to say, that our complaints against Mexico were fictitious or exaggerated? Under the commission extorted from her, without which, an open rupture must have followed, after ascertaining three millions of just claims, an amount much larger was left unadjusted, in consequence of the expiration of the time limited for the duration of the commission, and even that time shortened one half by the delays of the Mexican commissioners. Instead of exacting payment at once, of the debt thus ascertained and admitted to be due, we showed her every indulgence, by consulting her convenience as to the time and mode of payment. That debt still remains unpaid, and the remaining claim unadjusted. Now, I would ask, whether, under the circumstances, she was not bound to keep open diplomatic relations for the purpose of providing payment for the amount due, and for a proper adjudication of the remainder? She has thought proper to take offence at the annexation of Texas, and to put an end to diplomatic relations, and of course, of peaceful negotiation on that, as well as on other subjects. The act of recalling a minister, and sending passports to the foreign plenipotentiary, according to the modern law of nations, is equivalent to an express declaration of war, and hostilities might be expected to follow as a matter of course.* It looks very much as if the annexation was merely

*See *Kent's Commentaries.*—"Since the time of Binkershock, it has been settled by the practice of Europe, that war may lawfully exist by a declaration which is unilateral only, *or without any declaration on either side.*" In the war between England and France in 1778, the first public act on the part of the English government, was recalling its minister, and that single act was considered by France as the breach of the peace between the two countries. There was no other declaration of war, though each government afterwards published a manifesto in vindication of its claim and laid hold of as a pretext to avoid paying her debts, and making compensatian for the wrongs she had perpetrated on our citizens. The elosing of diplomatic relations was itself a great outrage, considering the relation in which she stood towards us. There was, certainly, no obligation on our part to take any step towards a renewal of those relations —we might have proceeded according to the usages of nations to take the law in our own hands, and compel her to give, what we might consider, a just indemnity. But unlike other nations, we pursued a humane and moderate course; we attempted again and again, to negotiate, but without success ; and perhaps, at the expense of national dignity· And even after the commencement of hostilities, after every success obtained by our army, the olive branch was held forth, and as often rejected.

It has been said, that the annexation of Texas by us was virtual war, that is, equivalent to an express declaration. If so, it was in consequence of the declaration of Mexico, that she would so consider it, but not as in its very nature precluding negotiation. On the contrary, the administration has been blamed for not negotiating, and that too, *whether Mexico would or not.* No—the act of war, was in closing the door to peaceful settlement, by means of plenipotentiaries, authorized to adjust not a single isolated question, *but all matters in dispute.*

A minister, clothed with full powers, was sent by us to Mexi-

conduct. The same things may be said of the war which broke out in 1793, and again in 1803.

The act of withdrawing a minister, is one of a most decisive character, for *actual hostilities* may exist without a state of war, as in the war of 1756 between France and England, and between us and France in 1798. The act of taking the fort of Mobile under Mr. Madison's administration in 1812, was an act of hostility, and yet our diplomatic relations still continued— it was made the subject of complaint by Spain, and defended or excused by our government. If diplomatic relations had been discontinued, there would have been no redress for Spain, but in returning the blow. Hence, I contend, that the party which closes these relations, and prevents the peaceful adjustment of injuries, is responsible for all the consequences.

co after the hasty and inconsiderate step taken by her, a piece of condescention, which can only be ascribed to an extreme desire on our part to preserve peace. Our plenipotentiary was not received, and for what reason ? Was it because be was not accredited, or not clothed with sufficient power to adjust *all* existing differences, the only grounds which could be fairly assigned ? No—the objection was, that these powers were *too full,* instead of being confined to one topic, the annexationof Texas. He was told, that a commissioner with powers to settle that single question, would be received, but without power to discuss any other, and consequently, without power to discuss even that, which was necessarily complicated with others. The representative, of course, could not divest himself of his powers— he went not only to do justice to Mexico, but demand justice of her. But, this is but a very imperfect view of the case. The willingness to receive *a commissioner,* went on the assumption, that we were in the wrong in the question of annexation, notwithstanding the ground taken by Mr. Webster, as Secretary of State, in his letter to Bocanega. Let us look at the letter of Pena y Pena, of the 15th October, 1845:

"In answer, I have to say to you, that although the Mexican nation is *deeply injured* by the United States, through the acts *committed by them in the department of Texas,* which belongs to this nation, my government is disposed to receive the commissioner *to settle the present dispute,* in a peaceful, reasonable, and honorable manner, thus giving a new proof, that even in the midst of its injuries, and of its firm decision to *exact adequate reparation* for them, it does not *repel* with *contumely,* the measure of reason and peace to which it is uninvited by its adversary."

It seemst hen, that Mexico does not *repel with contumely,* the commissioners sent to make *ample reparation* for the wrong done her in the department of Texas! The wrong done, *is to be taken for granted,* not to be discussed ; the *measure of repa-*

ration only, is to be debated. It is impossible to conceive of any thing more humiliating and insulting, whether it proceed from design or stupidity. A high minded nation could not brook such arrogance for a moment, and this from a power which admitted herself to be our debtor to the amount of millions which she is unable to pay! It would have been much more in place, for our minister to say, that the payment of that debt ought to precede any demand for *reparation,* on account of the alleged injury from annexation of Texas. I verily believe, that Mexico is the only power in the world to whom we should permit such language. At her instance, we had previously withdrawn our squadron from her coast ; and now, forsooth, she condescends to permit us to ask her forgiveness, and make ample reparation for what she pleases to consider the injuries done her in her department of Texas.*

Letter 12.

Struggle between Santa Anna and General Taylor.—The turning point of the War.

March, 1847.

The accounts from the seat of war in the States of the Rio Grande, are becoming every day more serious ; perhaps, I should say, alarming. It is now placed beyond all doubt, that Santa Anna, instead of throwing himself between the city of Mexico and the expected march of General Scott, has suddenly advanced on General Taylor at Saltillo. We now see the

* The battles afterwards fought, appear to have enlarged the vision of our enemy. No objections in the subsequent attempts at negotiation with Mr Trist, were alleged against his too ample powers. She was willing to yield California for a consideration, and Texas, with the boundary of the Nuesees, then mentioned for the first time ; and provided, slavery was not introduced in the ceded territories, and provided, also, that *religious toleration* were secured ! No one, after this, will deny, that the war has been productive of something to compensate for its horrors.

effect of weakening the army of the Rio Grande, under the supposition, that the Mexican Commander could make no other military movement than that of covering the national capital. The American General, by extraordinary exertion, has collected all his disposable force at the point where he can most advantageously arrest the march of Santa Anna; but his division does not exceed five thousand men, not more than half of them regulars, while the Mexican army is not short of twenty thousand, and by far the most formidable ever yet embodied in that country. We have every confidence in General Taylor and his gallant officers and soldiers; he is one of those, whose resources of mind have always been brought out by emergencies, and always found equal to them; but it must be confessed, the odds, at present, are fearfully against him.

It is said, that General Taylor has received orders (perhaps discretionary) both from the war department, and the commander in chief, to retreat to Monterey. This, I am confident, he will never do. He must meet Santa Anna on the edge of the desert of three hundred miles, which he is compelled to cross, and he will make his stand at the admirably chosen battle field of Buena Vista, which, according to the description of Captain Hughes, is a defile just suited for an army like that of General Taylor [to defend, and to withstand the shock of an attacking force, four times its numbers. Here is exactly one of those cases, where every thing must be put to "the hazzard of the dye," or every thing must be lost.

Let us for a moment consider the consequences of the retreat of General Taylor to Monterey or of his defeat at Buena Vista. Santa Anna once at Saltillo, will find every thing necessary to refresh his troops, after the sufferings and fatigues of their march. The retreat of the American General will be regarded as a victory for Santa Anna, and it will cause the rancheros of New Leon, Coawilla, and Tamaulipas, to rise *en mass* General Urrea, it is said, is at the head of ten thousand men near Victoria, so that our army will be shut up in Monterey, and all communications cut off with the Rio Grande. It is true, a portion of General Taylor's force may be detached to defend some narrow pass between Monterey and Saltillo, and attempt to oppose the advance of Santa Anna. But may not Monterey be turned by Urrea, and thus place himself in the rear of that detachment, while a portion of the Mexican army shall advance in front? Although Santa Anna may not be able to transport his artillery, is it impossible for him to enter the valley of the Rio Grande with his infantry and cavalry, by some circuitous way? I set up no pretensions to being a military critic ; my suggestions are merely thrown out for what they are worth, and they may be worth nothing. But I can conceive it possible, for Santa Anna, with his whole army, to enter New Leon and Tamaulipas, and the necessary consequence must be, that all our military stores at Comargo and Matamoras, must fall into his hands. He will sweep the whole valley of the Rio Grande, and in all probability, will not stop there, but cross into Texas, now almost defenceless, there being no force at any point capable of opposing his progress. Admit that these are bare possibilities, these may become probabilities, and probabilities, may become realities.

The supposed retreat, or defeat of our army, will change the whole face of the war. Should either of these events take place, (and such is my confidence in General Taylor, that I firmly believe they will not) then the descent on Vera Cruz, and the march to Mexico, under the commander in chief, will have to be abandoned, and a retrograde movement undertaken to the Rio Grande, which cannot be effected without great difficulty and delay.

Very serious charges have been made against the administration for aiding the return of Santa Anna to Mexico. I look upon this as an error on the part of Mr. Polk, and as a proof of his extreme desire for the restoration of peace. The favor

shown to the Mexican President, it was thought, would be followed by treaty; but the suspicious position in which he would
be placed before his own countrymen, would compel him to
prosecute the war with extraordinary vigor. It would only be,
after a series of glorious victories, and the expulsion of the
invaders by force of arms, that he could venture to talk of peace.

Our whole country waits with breathless auxiety, the issue
of the conflict between General Taylor and Santa Anna. It is
the turning point of this war—if our arms prove successful,
there will be every thing to hope, and peace will have been
conquered; but if we fail, the prospect before us will be dark
and gloomy indeed.*

LETTER 13.
The battle of Buena Vista, and its results.

APRIL, 1847.

SIR : We have at length authentic accounts of the great
battle fought at Buena Vista ; it is certainly one of the most
extraordinary on record, and its consequences are even more
important than the event itself. These are of such magnitude,
that Santa Anna never would have made his daring movement
if he had not been certain of success. Who could have supposed that twenty thousand men, under a high state of discip-
line, and perfectly provided with every thing necessary to constitute an army, cavalry, artillery, and infantry, should be totally
defeated by two thousand five hundred regulars, and an equal
number of volunteers? Such an idea certainly never entered
the mind of any Mexican, at least. It appears that his army
is entirely disorganized, and it is doubtful, whether he will
ever be able to reach San Louis with the fourth of those who

* This letter was not published in the series—after being transcribed for
publication, the copy was thrown into the fire, as presenting too discouraging a picture.

9

marched from that place. But the moral influence throughout Mexico must be incalculable—the Mexicans may now say as the subjects of Montezuma said of the Spaniards: "the gods of the strangers are stronger than our gods."

The reliance of the Mexicans for the defence of the Capital is destroyed and gone. Had Santa Anna been successful against Taylor, no other defence of the Capital would have been necessary; the descent on Vera Cruz would have been at once abandoned, and our troops recalled for the purpose of covering our own frontier. Instead of being broken and dispirited, the Mexicans every where, would have risen up in arms, and, perhaps, would for the first time, have exhibited a national spirit—the contrary of this effect has been produced. It will require a prodigious effort, and much time, to organize another army; and the greater part will be new conscripts, if they can be dignified even with that name, where there is no voluntary enlistment, or fair and regular draft, but where the poor peasant is seized by force, and driven, tied with ropes, to the places of rendezvous, like a brute beast, to be beaten, and broken into the trade of war. And now from Tampico to Saltillo, from the Sierra Madre to the Sabine, the war is over—*all that is necessary is to consolidate the conquest of the beautiful country west of the Rio Grande.*

I can readily conceive the effect of this uninterupted series of successful military events, and extraordinary battles, both on the Mexican and the European mind. The slumbering military might existing in our republic, ready to be called forth by events, must strike Europeans with amazement; and its secret lies in the freedom of our institutions, the same which gave to Greece and Rome their pre-eminence. One trait has been exhibited, in even a higher degree, than in Greece—the emulation or rivalry of States; and even of a higher kind than that which was displayed at Platea and Marathon; Kentucky has vied with South Carolina, and Massachusetts with Mississippi—

MAY THE CHERISHED REMEMBRANCE, LONG SERVE TO BIND
THEM TOGETHER IN FRATERNAL AFFECTION! The battles of
Palo Alto and Resaca, were decisive as to the superority of
our arms, especially of our artillery, and of the inferiority of the
enemy in cavalry, whose efficiency was so much overrated. At
Monterey, with every advantage of numbers, walls, and for-
tresses, they were literally crushed; and then, to crown all, at
Buena Vista, in spite of the immense disparity, and the enemy
attacking, their army was annihilated in the open field. Can
it be possible that Mexico will not now sue for peace, and accept any terms we may choose to dictate? I have no doubt
we shall soon hear of General Scott making good his landing
at Vera Cruz, and taking the Castle of San Juan. We shall
then hear of Mexican plenipotentiaries advancing towards him
with the olive branch, before he takes up his line of march for
the capital of the Astecs. Surely they will not invite him, " to
revel in the halls of the Montezumas."

It must be admitted, that Santa Anna, however detestable
his character, has displayed great military talent. He led his
troops to battle under circumstances, he was well aware, would
cause them to fight with desperation. They were not only
filled with confidence from their immense superiority of numbers,
but rendered desperate by hunger and the hope of booty, which
he had promised them, and which supplied the want of higher
motives of action, such as inspired the superior race with which
they had to contend. In the words of Byron:

"Th'Assyrian came down like a wolf on the plain,"

but the shepherd was prepared to receive him, and drive him back
howling to the desert. The sudden retreat of General Taylor
from his advanced position to his chosen battle ground, no doubt
unexpected, must have had the effect of disconcerting the enemy.
By thus meeting him at the edge of the desert, he availed himself, like a skilful commander, of all the advantages of circum-

stances. What events the war may bring forth, if it should continue, it is impossible to foretel, but it is certain, that the series of victories which have been thus far achieved by him, have not been surpassed in our military history, while that of Buena Vista, stands unequalled.

LETTER 14.

Shall we organize Territorial Governments in the conquered Territories.

MARCH, 1847.

Both political parties seem to take it for granted, that anexation must immediately follow the conquest of the whole or any portion of Mexico, by which is meant, the formation of new States to be added to the confederacy. But this is by no means a necessary consequence. Louisiana was not brought within the pale of the Constitution for eight years; Missouri for a longer time, and Florida for sixteen. They were placed under a first, and then a second grade of territorial government, over which the Constitution was not extended; rather their Courts, executive, judicial, or legislative branches, were not constitutional authorities, but depending on Congress for their being and power. It has been argued, that the acquisition of territory, either by purchase or conquest, (to which the same reason applies,) is not constitutional; and of this opinion, were Mr. Jefferson, John Quincy Adams, and I think I may add, Mr. Madison. But public opinion, and public necessity, have overruled them, not by fair reasoning, but by "jumping to the conclusion."

Under the territorial government, the territory has no vote in Congress, and no representation in the Senate, although allowed a delegate on the floor of the House of Representatives, with the liberty of speech, but without the right to vote. The territories of Louisiana, Missouri, and Florida, had their own legislatures, retained their own laws, and enacted new ones, but in this case, subject to the repealing power of Congress. They had also their own judiciary, with the exception of the Judges of the Superior Court, who, together with the Executive, were appointed under the organic law by the President of the United States ; that organic law, emanating from Congress, and which was for the territories, what State and United States constitutions, were for the States, might have given the power to the territories to elect their Governors and Judges, as well as their Legislators. This was in the pleasure of Congress, which had acquired the rights of the former sovereign, and might exercise it under the *limitations* of the Constitution, not because it was extended to the acquired territories, but as a restraint on Congress in its own sphere of action ; and whatever Congress was expressly forbidden to do generally, it was forbidden to do in any case, unless the exception was express. The organic law or territorial constitution, extended the great prerogative writs of *habeas corpus, mandamus,* and *quo warranto,* for the benefit and safe guard of persons, property, and religion of every citizen. The Government of each territory, as to all local subjects of legislation, was as completely at their own hands, as any of the States. Bnt has not Congress power of regulation over local subjects ? I do not find it in the Constitution, excepting over its real or moveable property. The District of Columbia stands on an anomalous principle ; and besides, in respect to that district, Congress acts in two distinct capacities : first, in its general character of a legislature for the whole Union ; and secondly, as a local legislature for the district ; and in this respect, the other States, have no more right to interfere, than they have a right to interfere with each other. Its local legislation, must be directed by its local wants, with which the people of Massachusetts or New York, have no concern.

The only acts of Congress extended to the territories are always expressly named, and they are those relating to the revenue, the slave trade, those regulating commerce and the public lands ; while the great body of the acts of Congress, have application only to the members of the confederacy. The general Government, in virtue of its sovereignty, had the control over all foreign intercourse, and undertook the military defence and protection. Having lived under these protective Governments, I must candidly confess, that they possess many advantages. They are entirely unlike the condition of colonies and conquered provinces, subject to onerous exactions, or restrictions. Their burthens were even lighter than those of the citizens of the States, in consequence of not being represented in Congress, as it would be against a fundamental principle to bind them by laws, which they had no share in enacting. Many of the territorial inhabitants regret the change from the quiet of their territorial Government, to the turbulence and expense of the State constitution. They preferred this state of things to the ambition of being able to disturb the balance of power among the States, by a voice in the Senate, or even in the House of Representatives. But the admission into the Union (or admission as States,) "as soon as consistent with the principles of the Constitution," was an express stipulation, under the treaties which ceded those territories ; and in the case of Texas, immediate annexation as a State, was the principal consideration of the compact. Where there is no such stipulation, as in the case of countries acquired by conquest, like those of the Rio Grande, the acquisition is unconditional, and the territorial state may be continued indefinitely, or the admission of the whole or part, be determined at our pleasure. According to the laws of nations, their local laws remain in force ; and according to our Constitution, Congress has no power to legislate in local matters for them, although it may create a local legislature for that purpose ; for, in my opinion, it cannot constitute itself a local legislature for the purpose, as in the anomalous case of the District of Columbia.

The Supreme Court is often regarded as the sole arbitor in

all constitutional questions. This is to be understood with some comitations. For instance, it would not consider itself at liberty to decide the question, whether the acquisition of foreign territory is constitutional or not; the other branches of the Government, the Legislation, the treaty making power, the Executive, having determined the high political question involved, the Supreme Court conforms to that decision. It, therefore, moves in a groove, and is not Supreme over all. Yet it has decided, in the case of Cairter, that the Courts of the territory are not constitutional Courts, and the Judges not constitutional Judges ; consequently its inferior Courts not inferior Courts of the United States.

We must distinguish between Political, and Municipal or local laws ; the former are abrogated *ipso facto*, by the charge of sovereignty, the later continue in force until repealed. For instance the whole body of the Spanish law was repealed in Louisiana, by an edict of Governor O.'Reilly, and in Missouri, the Spanish code, continue to Paris and we, were abrogated by the Governor and Judges, under the first grade of Government, and the common law with the statutes of one of the States, substituted in their place. One of the earliest decisions of the Supreme Court, was that the United States had no code of municipal law, but must resort to the municipal law of the State in which it happened to sit.

Let us suppose the whole of Mexico conquered by our arms, it may be divided, in the first instance, into four or five territories, which may be retained in that form of government at least as long as Florida, and be, afterwards, admitted as States, or be permitted to establish independent governments, bound to us by treaties of alliance, offensive and defensive. I hold it as a settled principle, that we cannot hold conquered countries like ancient or modern nations ; and we cannot, without violating the spirit of our institutions, deny them the right of self-government, or at least, of representation. The conquests we may make, cannot fail to better the condition of the conquered, by affording them better political institutions than those they before possessed. Surely, nothing can be worse than the present military anarchy of Mexico. They would obtain security for their rights, and obtain new ones, which they never enjoyed before; they would have peace within their borders, and safety from without. We should repel with indignation, the terms of reproach heaped upon us by the "tory" paper of England, the "Times." Our free governments carry blessings with them wherever they appear. Plunder and devastation, form no part of the American character, as is proved by the progress of our arms, marked by a degree of humanity unexampled in the annals of war and conquest. The affectation of concern for their religion, manifested by the Mexicans, is truly ridiculous in those who tolerate no religion but that of the State.

The subject of slavery is one of local, that is, of State or territorial legislation, except as to the foreign slave trade, which belongs to Congress in the regulation of foreign commerce. In the territory Northwest of the Ohio, there could not be said to be any system of law, it being uninhabited, or at least, the population was so inconsiderable, that it was not taken into consideration in establishing the ordinance of 1787, before the adoption of the present Constitution. It is in the nature of a compact between the States, and is not a case in point. But in Louisiana, the institution of slavery was already there, and could not be destroyed without interfering with a subject of local regulation of those territories, together with other subjects of domestic concern. Congress reserved to itself only a right to repeal, resembling a veto, except that the laws enacted continued in force until repealed; but, in no instance did Congress take the initiative in this local legislation. We may often discover the best expositions of the power of the Government, or any branch of it, by strict enquiry into the history of its practical operation.

Suppose the laws of Mexico *prohibit* slavery, would the simple repeal of the laws *establish* it? I do not see by what reasoniug it would do so. Is it probable, I would almost say possible, that slavery will be introduced by positive enactment? This would not only be local legislation, and on that account objectionable, even if it were possible, *as Congress is at present constituted.* It is said to be carried there by the Constitution. How can this be, if the Constitution does not extend there? A part cannot be extended without extending the whole. Congress is forbidden by the Constitution to legislate on certain subjects. This is true, but it is a limitation on its own powers, the effects of which are felt by the territories, as well as the States, but is no argument to prove, that the Constutition extends to the former as well as to the latter. I cannot see by what reasoning the Constitution is extended to them, and yet, I can readily see many curious, inconvenient, and unjust consequences arising from this view of the subject. It is impossible to avoid snch consequences, when we attempt to reason from false premises. We have started wrong in acquiring territory, when such acquisition was not contemplated by the Constitution; and that error is the cause of other errors. I see no way of surmounting these difficulties, but by mutual forbearance, reciprocal respect for each others feelings and interests.*

*The claim of the right to go to the acquired, or conquered territories with their slave property, is insisted on by the South. The attempted exclusion creates strong feelings, as it is regarded as offensive and unjust. If, according to my view of the subject, the conquered or acquired territory, is neither a part of any State, nor a part of the Union, the sovereignty is either in Congress, or in the inhabitants. According to European reasoning the sovereignty is in the Government; according to ours it is in the inhabitants; because with us, power travels upwards from the people, but according to the old reasoning, instead of ascending, it descends. But, if it be *assumed*, that the Constitution follows our flag, even if it be to the Typce Islands, then it would appear to me, that no citizen can be directly, or indirectly, excluded, on account of his carrying with him, persons *bound to service*, for that is

Much has been said on the subject of the laws of Mexico abolishing slavery, and no little merit is ascribed to her for her course on this head. When her pretensions are examined, it will be seen, that she is entitled to no credit whatever. African slavery was not introduced into that country, because the native indians, who had been reduced to a real bondage, already formed a cheaper slavery, than the African. In the

a condition, or relation recognized by the Constitution. Such servants are recognized if not as *property*, for taxation, yet as *persons* for representation. If the Constitution comes in conflict with the local laws, the latter must give way; this is the necessary consequence it is contended of extending the Constitution to the territories. Laying aside all this fine spun reasoning, there is a common sense ground of justice and equal right, in the claim to equal participation in the property acquired by common means, and even the appearance of the denial, must be offensive. The party thus denied, might exclaim " if it be arsenic, I will have my share."

The necessity of some legislation for the new territories, is evident, even if the first, or second grade of government, be not given to them. They are but *fragments* of other governments, depending on their superior, and their organization incomplete, when cut off from that superior. The jurisdiction of their courts was limited, or subject to appeal; their political, and military offices, acted under the order of their chief. The President of the United States as commander in chief, would command the military; but the United States judiciary could not entertain appeals, without authority of Congress; and neither could the President exercise civil control, without the same authority. The organic law, provides for the trial by jury, for the security of person, and conscience, not provided for in despotic countries. The laws regulating intercourse with the indians, the Post office, and many and on other subjects require to be specially extended. It is possible that by some indispensable legislation of this kind, the new acquisition, may get along for a while, by supplying the deficiency out of that original stock of power, which men possess in a state of nature, when compelled to do so by necessity. The attempt was made in Florida during a short interval, and it gave rise to much animadversion. I admit, that it may be in some manner obviated, by special legislation on the part of congress, if *from any cause*, it should be deemed inexpedient to establish territorial governments, even of the first grade. In Louisiana as in Florida, a Governor was appointed, clothed with the powers of the late Captain General, until Congress could act.

time of the conquerors, *villages* and *districts* were granted to them, the soil being only of secondary consideration. Their inhabitants were condemned to the severest labor, and were, in fact, slaves. The Spanish monarchs struggled with the wealthy proprietors to alleviate the condition of the unfortunate indians, and with success, so far as to rescue them from their original servitude; but, they are, at this day, little better off. Under the system of peonage, and the authority exercised by the alcades, their freedom is but nominal. This kind of slavery *is not abolished*; and as to abolishing negro slavery, it scarcely existed there. According to Mr. Ward, a few negroes were introduced about thirty years ago, but on finding the Indian labor much cheaper, they were suffered to go where they pleased. The only slavery in Mexico, except peonage, was in Texas.* This system is founded on a law of the *Siete Partidas*, which exempts females, ecclesiastics, military persons, scholars, and *gentlemen*, (hidalgos) from imprisonment, or liability of person, for debt! The poor Indian is, therefore, the only subject for the law to operate on. This kind of slavery commands the labor of the adult laborer, without the burthen of the aged and helpless, as is the case of negro slavery, which is not only a *relation*, but a *community*, where the able-bodied provide for the helpless. This pretention to merit on account of the abolition of slavery, is only an after thought arising out of the hostility to Texas. It was a subject of State legislation as with us, until the Mexicans

* It is not long, since a list of the peons who had escaped from the other side of the Rio Grande was published, and bitter complaints made by their masters to the Mexican Government, which was petitioned for redress! It is said that some proprietors own thousands, and they are a part of their estates. It is probable that neither slavery nor poenage can continue on the borders of the Rio Grande. During our military operations a large number of persons were freed by earning the means of paying the debts for which they were bound.

found that they could make capital out of it with our aboli-
tionists, and their English coadjutors. I detest hypocrisy,
and never was there any thing of this kind more palpable,
than the affectation of hostility to slavery by *Mexican philanthropists!* In enumerating the causes of difference between Mexico and Texas, I passed this topic in silence, because,
know it to be hollow and insincere, when put forth by a country
where human rights are held so cheap.

APPENDIX.

[*From the Republic.*]

Messrs. Editors: Some time last Spring, I published in the "Commercial Journal," of Pittsburgh, some views on the subject of the California
gold region, which have been confirmed by observations on the spot, published in the '*Alta California,*" and by accounts still more recent from that
country.

In order to understand the views referred to, it is necessary, in the first
place, to give a sketch of the geological features of the country·   A valley
of six hundred miles in length, and from fifty to a hundred in width, is formed
by the Sierra Neveda, or Snowy range on the east, and by the coast range
on the west.   This valley is watered by two rivers, the Sacramento and the
San Joachim; one rising due north, the other due south, and running towards each other; after uniting their waters they enter the bay of San
Francisco, which partly bounds the western side of the valley.   These rivers
may be said to wash the base of the Sierra Neveda, their waters being supplied,
almost exclusively, by streams which take their rise in that range of moun_
tains.   In this manner they form a continued line althongh coming from
opposite diections, receiving the drainings and detritns brought [down by
the innumerable torrents which cut the sides of the Sierra.   The alluvial
and diluvial deposites are, therefore, almost exclusively on the eastern side ;
and this accounts, also, for the overflow of the river on that side.   On looking at the map of Colonel Fremont, I was struck with the extraordinary
number of these ravines.   They look like so many streaks on the map, or,
rather, lines drawn by artificial agency ; but that agency is the sudden melt-
ing of the snows, and heavy rains of that climate.   One cause of this great
quantity of water discharged by the short mountain torrents, is the want of

sufficient elevation of the mountain, in that latitude, to retain the snows until they can melt gradually, as is the case of the Andes of Peru and Chili; and yet sufficiently elevated to receive a great depth of snow. This, when melted by the rains, rushes down with great force, carrying detritus along with it, and cutting through all the incumbent strata, until it reaches the level of the rivers, although still above the trap, or granite, which forms the nucleus of the mountain.

As this detritus is carried down, it becomes more and more disintegrated, until its further progress is arrested by the course of the rivers before mentioned, and is at last deposited in fine sand and gravel. The metalic threads are found, probably, not less than one-third of the way up the mountain; and if a shaft were sunk at the base of the mountain, it would have to go a depth before reaching the vein, corresponding with its present elevation above the original level. The metal, therefore, will only be found in these alluvial deposites, not beyond twenty or thirty feet in depth, formed in the course of time by the descending torrents. The nearer the river, and the farther from the seam, the finer will be the particles of gold; and the higher up the coarser, and less separated from the quartz in which it is detained. The most expensive part of mining, reducing the quartz to sand by stamping, the amalgation with quicksilver, and the separation of these by distillation, is thus saved, and the gold obtained with comparatively little expense. The stamping, or breaking up of the quartz, is performed by the natural agency of the water, and by the rocks falling upon each other in the course of their descent. Until these deposites shall be partially exhausted, although a much more precarious pursuit than regular mining, the latter will not be generally resorted to. There is no doubt, also, that others, with more perfect machines for washing and amalgamation, will follow those pioneers, and wash the same earth and sand over again, to as great profit as at the first operation. When I examined the lead mines of Missouri, I found that those who came after the regular smelters, took their scoria and leavings, and extracted, by means of the ash furnace, about twenty-five per cent., in addition to the firty already obtained, but without the expense and uncersinty of mining, which rendered it a sort of gambling pursuit.

Having giving this brief description, I will now proceed to what may be called theory—that is. *facts derived from induction.* Let us suppose a series of horizontal strata, one above another, but of unequal depth, incumbent on the original unstratified mass, which forms the nucleus of the globe. According to geologists, this was the natural position. Now, in consequence of some powerful voleanic agency, the lower mass is thrown up from below, and becomes the nucleus of a mountain, and that which was before the lowest, now appears at the top, while the various strata which lay flat upon it are tilted up on its sides. These being cut through, in the manner described, there is exposed to view in these cuts, the various strata and their contents, in the same manner as if a shaft had been sunk through them in their horizontal position. If there be any metallic seams to the right or left of these cuts, they will be seen like threads, and running lengthwise with the range of mountains. The metals contained in the now vacant spaces of these ravines, have been carried away and deposited below. The masses, thus broken and separated, have been still further reduced in the manner before stated, greatly diminishing the labor of mining. The deposits of detritus intermixed with gold may be the work of thousands of years; but the quantity may be estimated by the number and width of the natural cuttings through the gold seams now disconnected. It is certain that the amount of gold at the bottom cannot exceed the amount carried down from these original deposites. Without assuming that the amount of gold deposited in the Sierra Nevada is actually greater than in the same range further south, its peculiar geological and geographical character, may be a reason why gold may be *found* in California in greater abundance than in any other part of the world. It is found along this whole range from Sonora to Chili, although in greater or less abundance; and there is no doubt that a variety of other metals will be met with, perhaps as valuable, when the passion for gold washing shall have somewhat abated. It is remarkable that gold has been found almost invariably on the western or Pacific side of the great range, while silver, copper, and lead are discovered on the eastern side, and at a much greater elevation. It is probable that, instead of gold, silver and copper exist on the eastern side of the Sierra Nevada, towards the great Basin. What a field for the mineralogist!

- But, by what process, or operation of nature, came these seams, or veins of gold or other metals, to be thus deposited? Was it by the agency of fire, or by water and alluvion? I think it probable that both may have been at work, being the two greatest solvents in nature, and, at the same time, the greatest chrystalizers. Perhaps metallic *ores* may be the work of alluvion, and the production pure *metallic* substances—that of heat. With respect to gold, I think the latter theory is the more reasonable, as it is always found in a pure state, while the quartz (or pure silex) in which it is contained may be alluvial, and one of the earliest deposites from the decomposition of the ancient unstratified mass. But where shall we seek for the original supply of the precious metal? How is it formed, or whence has it been extracted by the agency of heat? It is not enough to say that, like other metals, it is found diffused throughout all nature, for an appreciable quantity of gold has been extracted from violets. In my opinion, it exists on the original unstratified mass, in imperceptible proportions; but those proportions varying in different places, other metals being more or less abundant. The greater proportion of our soils, according to Sir Humphrey

Davy, is formed by the decomposition of the original granite; and this accounts for diffusion of gold in minute particles, which may be taken up by plants, and enter into the composition of organized bodies. If then, the unstratified rock is the original seat of the metal, but in particles infinitely minute, it may have been separated by a very high degree of heat, by which it would be sublimated or volatilized, and thus carried upwards by chemicoelectric force, by a process resembling distillation. In this way, it would penetrate the quartz rock, or be condensed in the spaces of the laminated strata, such as the talc, schist, or mica slate. Such is the theory of Trimmer, Buchland, and other modern mineralogists. Lyell says—"granite, syenite, and those porphyries, which have a granite form structure, in short all plutonic rocks (rocks having undergone the action of heat) are frequently observed to contain metals, at or near their junction with stratified formations. On the other hand, the veins which traverse stratified rocks are as a general law, more metaliferous near such junctions, than in other portions. Hence it has been inferred that these metals may have been spread in a *gaseous form*, through the fused mass, and that the contact of another rock, of a different state of temperature or sometimes the existence of rents in other rocks in the vicinity, may have caused the sublimation of the metals."

One thing is certain, as may be at once seen by those who have examined the larger masses of gold brought from California, that the finer particles of gold have been run together, by a second operation of heat, sufficient only to fuse them and separate them from the quartz. The first was distillation, the second smelting, or rather simple fusion. It is possible that these great operations of nature have been repeated at different intervals, and different seams of quartz and gold, may be found in ascending the ravines; the lower, more completely scattered (but in finer particles) through the quartz, and the higher having afterwards undergone simple fusion.

I think it premature to offer any conjecture as to the amount of gold which may be expected from California; but I cannot but think that it will be sufficient to produce a perceptible effect on its commercial value. According to Mr. Prescott, the sudden influx of gold from Mexico and Peru reduced its value, as compared to commodities, about two-thirds in the course of twenty years. A new stimulus has been given to the pursuit of gold mining throughout the world, in consequence of the discoveries of our enterprising countrymen in Califoania. The extraordinary increase of gold in the Bank of England may be an indication that its value is decreasing as compared to silver, and therefore less desirable for hoarding. It is certain that it is a less perfect standard of value than silver, the latter being also a scarce metal, compared to other metals, but a better representative than gold, of the labor and capital expended in its production, while gold has been repeatedly thrown into circulation in sudden and unlooked-for quantities, I would instance the amount of gold found in Calcutta on its capture by Clive—an amount, although imperfectly known, admitted to have been immense. We may expect that the gold mines of Siberia, of Brazil, of Mexico and Southern America, of the eastern and even western parts of Europe, Hungary Transylvania, Silesia, of Spain, and even of Norway and Sweden, as well as of the Appalachian, in our southern States, will awaken new efforts of combined skill, labor, and capital.

H. M. BRACKENRIDGE.

THE EARLY DISCOVERIES OF THE SPANIARDS IN NEW MEXICO.

Messrs. Editors: One of the most difficult things I ever undertook has been to trace the different journeys of discovery of the Spaniards, in the country to which they gave the name of New Mexico; and it would have been impossible to have accomplished this undertaking, but for the assistance of that extraordinary and invaluable collection of maps and books on the subject of America, made with great expense and labor, by Mr. F. Box, of Washington. Of these difficulties no one can form a just idea who has not made the attempt. It may be proper to state, that the whole country, from the mountains east of the Rio Grande to the Pacific—from about 32° south to 37° north—iu consequence of these discoveries, and on account of its great cities, and its numerous and civilized population, was called New Mexico in reference to old Mexico, as New Spain was named in reference to old Spain. My principal source of information is the work of Gomara, and Hackluyt's collection of voyages; but I was obliged to consult many other works.

In some of the oldest maps, the Colorado of California is called the *Rio Grande del Norte*, and is represented as taking its rise in a great lake to the north east; while the *Rio Grande of the Gulf*, or, as it was called, the North Sea, does not appear. It will be readily seen that this was sufficient to account for much of the confusion and mistakes of the early writers, and of the fruitless attempts to trace the early journeys of discovery.

'The first journey was that of Marco de Nicia, a friar, accompanied by a small party. He set out from Pitatlan, on the Gulf of California, in latitude 24°, in the year 1539, about twelve years after the conquest. I shall not enter into details. After some days' travel to the north, through populous countries, he came to Vacupa, where he first heard of populous countries to the north, of the province of Cibola, and of the seven great cities. After reaching, as he supposed, latitude 26°, he found indians who had no knowledge of Christians. He was then about fifty leagues from the Gulf of California. He was informed by these indians of a great plain, about thirty days' further travel to the north, inhabited by people living in large towns, built of stone and lime, who wore cotton garments, and possessing abundance of gold and turquoises, sometimes called *emeralds*, from the affinity to that precious stone.

Advancing still further, he sent a negro and some indians to see and report to him on their return, while he followed them slowly. Some of these indians returned, and informed him that they had reached Cibola, but had been badly treated, and the negro killed. Nicia, on his return, wrote his account[1] which is, in many respects, exaggerated and fabulous; It gave rise, however, to an expedition under Vasques de Coronado, in 1540. Coronado was greatly disappointed, and freely gives the lie to the accounts of Nicia. He went as far as the cities of Cibola, which he described as consisting of five small towns, of five hundred houses each, well built of stone, He heard of populous provinces to the north, and of cities on a great salt lake, to the northwest, where there was an abundance of gold. The lake was probably the Pacific Ocean. It is remarkable that nearly all the tribes on the Atlantic slope had a vague notion of the Pacific, and supposed it to be at a short distance from them. He returned with the intention of making another expedition, but which he never accomplished. The towns which he saw, were, no doubt, near the Gila, and south of that river, while the great province of Cibola lay to the north between that river and the Colorado. The unfavorable report of Coronado, and the failure of Cortez in his northern explorations, had the effect, no doubt, of discouraging further discoveries in this direction.

No further attempts were made to explore the country for nearly forty years. In the mean time, the Spanish settlements had advanced from Guadelaxara to New Biscay, and the valley of St. Bartholomew, or Chiwawa. In the year 1583, a well prepared exploring expedition was set on foot, under the command of Antonio de Espejo. It proceeded north to the Conchas and Pasaguetas, numerous tribes, who had no previous knowledge of the christians. Their course was along the Conchas.

They followed the river to the Tobosos and Jumanos, where they found large towns, with flat roofs, built of stone and lime, and regularly laid out in streets. They now reached the *Rio Grande of the Gulf of Mexico*—here is a point of departure about which there can be no mistake. They proceeded about twelve days up the river, and came to another great nation. The inhabitants wore mantles of cotton with blue stripes, of handsome fabric. I have no doubt this was the present *Paso del Norte*. After leaving this, they travelled fifteen days up the river, through a country not admitting of population, and this is its present character, until they came to what may be called the valley of Santa Fe. They found towns with houses four and five stories high, warmed by stoves, and ladders to ascend from one story to the other. They proceeded thence to Tiguasi, where they found sixteen towns. Here they learned that the eastern part of Cibola bordered on this province, the western border of which had been visited by Coronado. They speak of eleven other towns containing forty thousand inhabitants. Whether they meant families (vicinos) or *souls*, I am unable to say. They proceeded up the Rio Grande to Cia, or Zia, the largest town they had seen, containing twenty thousand inhabitants and eight market-houses. The houses were plastered and handsomely painted, and the people civilized. At this place, hearing of a great province to the northwest, they took that direction. They heard of seven large towns, but did not go to see them. Fifteen leagues further, still going west, they came to a great town called Acoma, situated on a high rock, accessible only by a way cut in the rock. The inhabitants were supplied with water by cisterns. Twenty-four leagues further, they came to the province of Zuni, called by the Spaniards Cibola, where the inhabitants had information of the visit of Coronado. They were informed that, at the distance of eighty leagues, there was a great lake, many large towns, and plenty of gold—probably California. The main party now returned towards the Rio Grande, while Espejo and nine companions went further west. After travelling twenty-eight leagues, they found a great province, containing fifty thousand inhabitants, called Zaguato. They heard much of the cities of the Great Salt Lake, the Pacific and their wealth, gold, &c. Espejo made an excursion of forty five leagues to the northwest, where it was said there were silver mines, and which he found very rich. This was near two rivers of *reasonable* size, probably the Colorado and the Jaguisita. I am satisfied that the country thus explored lay between the Gila and the Colorado.

On the return of Espejo, the main party determined to return to New Biscay, or Chiwawa, but he resolved to ascend higher up the river. The only mention of degrees of latitude is on one occasion, when they speak of having reached the 37th degree; but this was probably mere guess-work.

Espejo now ascended the river sixty leagues to Quires; thence, going east, he came to Hubites, containing twenty-five thousand inhabitants, and he heard of the Tamas, containing forty thousand. Whether these were towns or provinces is not stated. All the places visited had gold, and turquoises, and manufactured fine cotton cloths. The myriads of buffalo, or crooked backed oxen, which covered the whole face of the country were mistaken for domestic herds; no country on the globe was ever so abundantly supplied with the means of subsistence through this animal, as were the aborigines of the interior of North America. So that particular districts might be most thickly populated, while vast unoccupied regions lay around them, swarming with the buffalo, or rather the bison, which is the true name of that animal. Their skins were elegantly dressed by them; and, for the finer kinds, the mountain sheep, or goat, or chamois, as the Spaniards called it, furnished an abundant supply. Espejo resolved to return by a different course, and was conducted by the indians down the *Rio de las Vacas* which he followed 120 leagues, meeting with no inhabitants, but vast numbers of *cattle.* But without seeing any habitations, the herdsmen appearing to live among their herds. The use of fire-arms has no doubt rendered them more shy, and at one time they literally blackened the face of the western prairies. Their range was limited both to the south and north. He then struck across to the Rio Grande, and came to the Conchas, by which he returned to New Biscay. The Rio de las Vacas is evidently the Rio Puerco, or Peqos. Here closses the expedition. Having the point of departure fixed, and at the same time the point of termination equally ascertained, I think the whole mystery of these expeditions has been cleared up.

The question will naturally present itself, what has become of the millions of civilized people who occupied New Mexico? I will ask, what has become of the millions of Yucatan, of Chiapas, and of Old Mexico? The reduction to slavery, their wars, and other causes, are not sufficient to account for the disappearance of the great nations of the west, or of the Atlantic slope. In looking for a cause, I have found one fully adequate, in that horrid plague and scourge, the small-pox. Let any one read the accounts of McKenzie, Carver, and Catlin, and I think he will seek no further for it. To the indian it is peculiarly fatal, not only from his want of skill in treating it, but from his physical organization; his skin is so remarkably thick that the pustules cannot break through it, and the disease is almost always fatal. When among the Arikaras, I was informed by them that they were but the remnant of seventeen towns lower down the river, and I traced their former abode for seven miles. The Arikaras and Mandans have since disappeared from the earth. After the greater part had been carried off by the small-pox, the survivers abandoned these towns and fled, covering their trails as they went, as if pursued by an enemy; but that mortal foe still followed them to annihilation. I have not been able to find any account of the nations of New Mexico from the year 1583 until 1698; and it is perhaps during that interval, that the rapid destruction of the American tribes and nations took place, while there was no one to record the desolation of the provinces of Cibola, or the country of the Buffaloe, which is the meaning of the word. The ruins of cities on the Gila, and between it and the Colorado, remain to prove the fact that they once existed. Yet, there are some remnants of their former civilization in the Nabahoes, and the Pumas one on the Gila, the other on the heads of the Colorado, who still live in well-built houses, and manufacture their beautiful blankets. The suggestion I have made might be extended to the old world, and its ruined cities of Asia and Africa.

The only recent account of the country between the Gila and the Colorado which I have been able to meet with, is in Pattie's Narrative, a hunter of Kentucky, who trapped on the Gila and Colorado twenty-five years ago, whose journal is done into readable English by the geographer, Flint. Pattie saw many of these ruins; saw much fine land heavily timbered; and by the friendship of the Nabahocs, was directed through a pass at the head of the Colorado which carried him to the Platt of the Missouri. This is, possibly, the pass sought for by Colonel Fremont. Pattie went through it in May; if it was bad then, what must it have been in the depth of winter! I am of opinion, that between 32° and 37° there is sufficient land to make two States, without going east of the Rio Grande del Norte. Yet, it was but partially seen by Pattie. It appears to be a mountainous country, well watered, and no doubt abounding in minerals, and having many rich valleys adapted to cultivation. The Colorado is a fine river, navigable eight hundred or a thousand miles with steamboats, unless there be obstructions that we do not know of. In extent, it is equal to Pennsylvania or Virginia. It will not be long before it will be thoroughly explored by our countrymen. Pattie says that it contains numeroes bands of the most savage and ferocious Indians, armed with bows and arrows pointed with flint, who have had no intercourse or knowledge of the whites. He says that the country in some respects reminded him of parts of Kentucky, his native State.

H. M. BRACKENRIDGE.

DESTRUCTION OF THE INDIANS BY SMALLPOX.

I could bring together numerous separate accounts of the fatal ravages of this disease among the Indians in different portions of the continent. Bernal Dias, *incidentally* mentions, that it carried off a *million* shortly after the conquest, but how many more we are not told. The disease, no doubt, appeared at different intervals. A sermon by a New England divine, (in the collection of Mr. Force) of 1621, mentions that not more than one in twenty of the natives then remained, the rest having been carried off by the small-pox. In a Jesuit account which I found in the same collection, it appears that it broke out among the Indians in Chiwawa in 1617, and carried off whole tribes of Indians. There was no escape from it, for as long as two remained together the contagion might be there; it was, therefore, more fatal than an atmospheric epidemic, which might be checked by change of place or season. The Indian fled from his village or town, and never returned to it; he never dared to approach it afterwards, believing it to be haunted by evil spirits. In many places, this superstitious dread prevails to this day.

McKenzie gives the following account of the destruction of the Knistenew and Chippowyen tribes in 1780: "This was the small pox which spread its destructive and desolating power, as the fire consumes the dry grass of the field. The fatal infection spread round with a baneful rapidity which no flight could escape, and with a fatal effect that nothing could resist. It destroyed with its pestilential breath whole families and tribes; and the horrid scene presented to those who had the melancholy and afflicting opportunity of beholding it, a combination of the dead, the dying, and such, as to avoid the horrid fate their friends around them, prepared to disappoint the plague of its prey, by terminating their own existence.

" The habits and lives of those devoted people, which provided not to-day for the wants of to-morrow, must have heightened the pains of such an affliction, by leaving them not only without remedy; but even without alleviation. Nought was left to those but to submit in agony and despair."

"To aggravate the picture, if aggravation were possible, may be added, the putrid carcasses which the wolves, with a furious voracity, dragged from the huts, or which were mangled within them by the dogs, whose hunger was satisfied with the disfigured remains of their masters. Nor was it uncommon for the father of a family whom the infection had not reached, to call them around him, to represent the crnel sufferings and horrid fate of their relations, from the influence of some evil spirit who was preparing to exterpate their race, and to invite them to baffle death with all its horrors, by their own poignards. At the same time, if their hearts failed them in this necessary act, he was himself ready to perform the deed of mercy with his own hand, as the last act of his affection; and instantly follow them to the common place of rest and repose from human evil.

" It was never satisfactorily ascertained by what means this malignant disorder was introduced, but it was generally supposed to be from Missouri by a war party."